# The
# Holitaph

# The Holitaph

Copyright © 2012 by Joe Cron

Cover image © Joe Cron

Cover image produced by
Joe J. Calkins, Cerberus Art, cerberusart.com

Second Print Edition: November 2013

Lardin Press
Everett, Washington
mail@lardinpress.com
www.lardinpress.com

ISBN-13: 978-0615926759
ISBN-10: 0615926754

This book is a work of fiction. Names, characters, places, and incidents depicted in this book are either products of the author's imagination or are used fictitiously. Any similarity to real persons, living or dead, is coincidental and not intended by the author.

# For Babs

*Thanks for reading everything.*

# THE HOLITAPH

# CHAPTER 1

The grey cubicle barriers on either side of the hallway formed a familiar corridor for Dylan Bruce as he arrived at the office in his signature denim jacket and brown leather fedora. Beneath, casual engineer attire, with jeans, a light blue, long-sleeved shirt, and white tennis shoes. He'd almost chosen a little more businesslike look with khaki slacks and dress shoes, because he had a customer meeting that morning, but in the end comfort won out.

Dylan was thirty-three, and a quality engineer at the plant. He was tall and thin, with chiseled features. He was one of those men who always seemed to have a three-day beard, as if he shaved every day, but with a razor set to leave stubble. His dark brown hair was long and somewhat disheveled, intentionally.

Dylan had a scruffy appeal that worked well for him, though he had also been long amused by people's reaction to his appearance. He got comments in school that he didn't look like a liberal arts student, and he got comments during his career that he didn't look like a quality engineer. He wasn't sure what he was supposed to look like, but it seemed whatever it was, he was some type of anomaly.

He was holding a flat, flimsy box and a bottle of ginger ale as he ran a finger along the cloth wall and turned a corner between the rat-maze panels. He plopped the box on the small, round table in the center of a cluster of four cubicle desks, then set the ginger ale on his desk.

"Hey, I smell doughnuts," said Matt Claremore, a mechanical engineer who sat next to Dylan. "Most excellent, dude."

Dylan enjoyed perking things up a little from time to time. His cubicle mates were a competent and reasonably entertaining bunch, despite the use of phrases such as "most excellent," and Dylan tried to occasionally remind himself that things could be a lot worse. Doughnuts were a recurring and not terribly creative perk, but they were still different than, and better than, nothing.

His company was Trocconics, a Detroit area electronics manufacturer making gauges and instrument panels for farm equipment, boats, and other types of vehicles. The offices were nothing special, a classic cubicle forest bathed in fluorescent overbrightness, with the faint aroma of copy machine. As Dylan pulled his chair away from his desk, another colleague, a short, puffy-blonded woman named Barbara Teunis, came around the wall in a lime green business suit, holding a greeting card.

"Oh, Dylan, y'all are here already. That's great," she said. "This card's goin' 'round fer Paul. He had hisself a accident, and he's over at Mercy."

"Oh, no," said Dylan, taking the card. "What happened? Car accident?"

"Nah, sumpin' with chemicals," said Barbara. "Some of us are headed yonder at lunch to visit and take the cawrd. Matt, you on here?"

"Yup," said Matt.

"I'll go with you," said Dylan, handing back the signed card. "Stop by here when you guys are headed out and I'll stow away with you."

"Awrahty," Barbara said, turning back down the hall. "Y'all be sweet."

"Want a doughnut?" Dylan asked.

"Wanna hawrt attack?" said Barbara as she walked down the hallway.

"Whatever," Dylan said to Matt. "Ever heard of a cop having a heart attack from doughnuts? Maybe they do down in Texas."

"She means the bacon, dude," Matt said. Dylan's favorite doughnut wasn't a doughnut at all, but a maple bar with bacon bits on top, and any box of pastries Dylan brought in always had at least four of those in it. Dylan wasn't unfit, but he did enjoy his bacon maple bars.

"Ah, crap," he said.

"What?" asked Matt.

Dylan had his hand in his jacket pocket. "Left my cell phone in the car," he said.

"You won't need it," said Matt. "You'll be in that thrilling design review all morning."

"Yeah, don't remind me," Dylan said.

He hedged a moment, then turned to leave. "I'll feel naked without it," he said. "Back in a sec."

He made his way back through the maze and out of the building, then across to the far edge of the asphalt parking lot. He preferred to park away from other cars, but not because he was trying to protect a fancy ride. He drove a 1970 Buick Skylark, and he loved it, but didn't obsess over it. He parked in the clear areas mostly because the lot lines were painted a bit small. A hefty stroll was a fine trade for squeezing in and out of the car, especially since a '70 Skylark had long doors and Dylan had long legs. He needed some decent space to swing open enough room to get out comfortably. Besides, it was a crisp, cloudless, autumn morning, the kind of day that made Dylan want to be out for a walk, regardless.

The plant was in a pleasant area outside the heart of town. There were trees dotting the company landscaping, and the property next to it was a cemetery, so there was plenty of open green. Inside the building was the same as being inside most any other manufacturing plant, but at least the outdoors didn't feel like the place was crammed into an urban industrial zone.

Dylan arrived at his car, opened it, and grabbed his phone from the small plastic tray he kept on the passenger seat.

He closed and locked the car, then stood a moment and took a big breath. The autumn air told him somebody somewhere was burning leaves. It made him think about grilling up a couple of hamburgers later for dinner. He fired up the grill less often than he used to, ever since his wife passed away. Today was a day for it, though, if ever there was one.

His thoughts lingered a moment on his late wife, Stephanie, as they still often did. He'd been married at twenty-three, ten years ago, and Stephanie died of a rare and aggressive cancer six years later. Even after four years without her, moving on with someone else hadn't worked out. He was certain in his own mind that he wasn't clinging to that memory too tightly, but the longer he stayed single, the more he wondered if he really just hadn't met the right woman yet. Maybe he was playing some other game in his subconscious.

Stephanie was tall and gorgeous, with long brown hair to go with captivating brown eyes. She was smart and fun. They were on a journey together, and shared a vision for their lives. Four years after she was gone, Dylan still had that vision in his head. They never had kids, and now Dylan wasn't sure if he wished they had, so he would have a child to carry on her legacy, or was glad they didn't, so he could freely move on. In theory, anyway.

He started back across the lot. About halfway between his car and the building, he thought he noticed the ground moving a little under him.  An earthquake.

Or not.

Within seconds, the pavement ten feet in front of him began to crack and heave, making a hill.  At first two feet high, then it pulsed and heaved to four feet high.  Dylan's instinct was to run, but the earth beneath him was too unstable.  He couldn't get his footing well enough and fell down, scrambling around to be able to watch what was happening.

The pavement heaved again to six feet.  The material crumbled apart into chunks of asphalt, as dirt was pushing up between the chunks.

Then, the hill got so large that Dylan was being lifted up with it.  The dirt erupted and flowed out of the hole, and Dylan saw what looked like some kind of animal skin coming up through it.

It was greenish and shiny.  Yes, it was definitely moving and coming up out of the hole.

It rose and showed itself as a tentacle, then two more tentacles, then part of the body.  It was so foreign it was hard to tell for sure, but it looked injured.  The skin was blistered in places, cracked and bleeding in others.

Dylan watched in amazement as the creature's body arose.  The three tentacles pushed against the cracked asphalt so as to lift its body out of the ground.

It had a head shaped like an enormous football, with two eyes the size of a normal football and a mouth six feet across. The torso was flatter than its head, and oblong, with ridges down its back.  The tentacles were attached to this torso, in an odd way that was not in any apparent pattern.  The whole animal looked like something a second-grader might draw, and Dylan thought it was really weird that a thing like that would cross his mind while this was happening.

Dylan really couldn't do anything but lie there in shock and think things like that.  It was so outrageous as to not even seem dangerous, in spite of the fact that he was clearly in much too close proximity to a creature capable of breaking through asphalt. And through a bunch of dirt below that, however deep it was.

It occurred to him again that this thing really looked to be in bad shape. All over it were welts and bleeding wounds, and it seemed to be getting worse right in front of him.

As if Dylan could get any more surprised, he quickly did. One of the creature's tentacles flung out and wrapped several times around his right wrist. Another of the tentacles reached toward him, but instead of grabbing him, uncoiled and placed a three-inch cube in the palm of his hand. It was made of some kind of stone or hard resin and was perfectly pitch black.

The instant it touched him, he felt at once like it was giving him a mild electric shock, but was also soothing and energizing.

Then, the being pulled him slightly toward its head and spoke. "Burba kikik."

The black cube burned his hand as the tentacles loosened, and Dylan dropped it immediately. The tentacles not only loosened, they began to decompose. The creature went completely limp and in a matter of seconds dissolved into a huge pile of green goo, which then evaporated into thin air.

No one else was in the parking lot. The fall breeze blew silently over the scene, with Dylan sitting in front of a large, motionless pile of freshly unearthed soil and pavement. Dylan looked at his hand, front and back. It felt normal and looked normal.

The impulse to run suddenly hit him, so he got up and took off.

He ran out of the parking lot and down the street, along the cemetery on the adjacent property, until he was over a small hill and couldn't see the parking lot or his plant building any more. It wasn't really very far, but this was pretty much a full sprint the whole way, so he was winded. He sat on the ground next to the sidewalk.

Compared to what just happened, things seemed blissfully

normal where he was.  He would find out later that they really weren't.  A fair number of people saw what happened, mostly from their cars, and there was a standstill forming in the traffic.  The impulse to run instead of trying to drive away was a good thing.  He was more mobile on his feet.

In the distance, sirens were blaring.  They were getting closer.

Dylan couldn't see whatever was happening in the company parking lot, but he didn't really care.  As far as he was concerned, he was now pretty much entitled to a day off and whatever the hell he felt like doing.  Some people in cars were yelling to him, asking if he was OK.  He ignored them. He got up and began walking down the street.  He felt pretty good.  Strangely good, in fact.

He watched with an odd sense of mild amusement as cars near him began slowing and stopping to allow the emergency vehicles past.  He found himself wondered what the e-vehicles were actually for.  Nobody got hurt.  No humans, that is. There weren't even any damaged cars in the parking lot, as far as he remembered.  There wasn't anything for police or fire or ambulances to do.  There was nothing but some dug-up asphalt.  He guessed someone must have called nine-one-one. Oh, well.

Dylan's head was swirling in a mix of invigoration and confusion.  In a scatterbrained state, his thoughts drifted around to anything that passed through his head.

He looked around at the trees in the cemetery and thought of how pretty they were in the fall.  He thought of a girl he wanted to date in high school, but never did.  What would have happened if he'd take her to the prom?  Whatever. He remembered playing with the slot car racing set he had as a kid.  Everything about it.  The whirring and buzzing sounds, sitting on the hardwood floor, smelling the electrical transformer that ran the game. Man, that was fun.

Ambling aimlessly down the sidewalk, Dylan found himself nonplussed by the events of the past ten minutes.

Through a combination of denial and bewilderment, he was quite calm. He decided he was hungry, and there was a greasy spoon about four blocks away. He'd never eaten there; he always drove past. Today was the perfect day to stop in and try their biscuits and gravy.

He took three more steps when a brilliant flash of light came out of the sky like a ball of lightning and hit the grass just to the left of him. It didn't have much of an impact and didn't kick up much dirt; it just sort of sizzled a moment with a little smoke. Then, there was nothing there but a small crater the size of a basketball. The grass was gone and there were brown clumps that looked for all the world like the dirt had been fused into globs of glass.

Dylan was shocked out of his serenity, but didn't have even a moment to react before another fireball instantly landed to his right.

It melted the curb.

He instinctively took off running again, hardly noticing the screaming people getting out of their vehicles and running the other direction. As he sprinted down the sidewalk, the lightning balls hit every few seconds, next to him or just behind him. They were following him!

He got to the next cross street, where some cars were moving slowly through the intersection. He ran out between them. There was honking and slamming of brakes, creating a clearing in the intersection. One of the fireballs hit a car and it exploded.

The explosion blew Dylan off his feet, and he rolled a couple of times on the pavement.

On his back, Dylan looked up into the sky and saw the fireballs coming from very far away, farther than he could see, and they seemed to come straight at him, then veer when they got very close. Four of them came in quick succession and blasted the pavement in a perimeter around him. Then they stopped.

Dylan took a breath and coughed on the fumes of

incineration. It occurred to him with some shock and dismay that whatever this twisted series of events was, it just took a turn. Someone was hurt now. That car exploded. Someone was dead.

The surroundings were total bedlam. People yelling, running, calling. A police car with lights blazing came to a stop in the intersection. The cop got out and cautiously stepped around the burning shell of the destroyed vehicle, as if to see if there was anyone there that could still be helped. There really wasn't the slightest chance of that.

Dylan was still basically on his back, but raised up on his elbows. Bits of debris were uncomfortable under his forearms, but he ignored that.

He hadn't gotten much of his wits about him yet, and the cop came over near him, but keeping his distance.

"What the hell is going on here?" he asked.

*If you're relying on me to know that*, thought Dylan, *we're all in very serious trouble*.

"What do you mean?" Dylan said.

"I mean I saw what was happening. Who the hell are you and what are you doing?"

"What...what am *I* doing?" Dylan asked.

The cop was extremely confused, and pulled his gun. "What's going on?"

The gun sent a bolt through Dylan's nerves, and he searched his thoughts frantically for an appropriate response. He didn't find one, but he answered the cop, anyway.

"If you saw everything, why are you asking me?" he said.

"I saw you running, explosions all around you, then this car blew up." He seemed to be coming to strange conclusions as he was speaking. "Whatever you did, you killed somebody."

"Are you *insane?*" said Dylan. "How could I do this?"

"Shut up!" the cop yelled. "Get on your stomach. Now!"

All the morning's occurrences to that point notwithstanding, being taken into police custody because of it was out of the question. Dylan was as law-abiding as anyone else, but this was different. He was ready to be as rebellious as he needed to be, and had no intention of allowing the cop to arrest him.

"Now!" the cop repeated. The scene was beginning to draw a scattered crowd of those too stunned to run away before this.

Dylan decided the cop was probably too scared and disoriented to actually shoot him if he bolted. He began to roll slowly over from his back to his stomach, but only until he was in a better position to spring to his feet. Once he had a hand and a knee properly positioned on the pavement, he made his choice.

He shoved himself up and got a foot under him to propel into a sprint.

But he was wrong about the cop. The policeman fired two shots without a thought.

Although the cop was only eight feet away, neither bullet struck Dylan, who was committed to his actions and was already running within another moment. He heard one of the shots striking the fender of a car, then some screaming from the bystanders. Dylan didn't hear the other one and didn't care.

All he knew was the instantaneous terror from being shot at, then the adrenaline-fueled realization that he was not hit. The onlookers were too confused by everything—including the cop's behavior—to react as though Dylan was a criminal, and within seconds he was half a block away and already among pedestrians who had no idea he was connected to the situation.

Dylan ran another block, until he was satisfied he was not being chased, and stopped to catch his breath again. Seems the cop didn't know what to make of his getaway. Fine by him.

He immediately noticed he was not as winded as before, when he ran from the company parking lot. At first, he bent

over and rested his hands on his knees.  Breath.  Breath.
Breath.

Then, he stood up straighter and lifted an arm to lean on
the orange brick wall of an old, three-story warehouse.  The
DeFarva Warehouse, he remembered.  Had been empty for a
couple years since the DeFarva company went under.

After a few seconds, he felt it begin to shake.

Dylan took his hand away and looked around, realizing
that the ground was not shaking.  He reached out and touched
the warehouse wall again, and it was vibrating vigorously.
Before Dylan could figure out how to react, glass burst from
every window in the building, and the brick walls began to
crumble apart.

Within seconds, huge chunks of brick were toppling
directly above him.

With no time to do anything else, Dylan instinctively
cowered and put his arms over his head.  He realized he was
still wearing his hat and strangely hoped it might somehow
help protect him.

Pieces of the walls began showering the sidewalk and
street around him, but nothing struck him.  He looked up and
saw a long blob of pink putty reaching up from behind him,
frantically poking and slapping at the falling bricks.  It
successfully pulverized or knocked them all away above his
head.

Within a few seconds, the entire building was rubble.

# CHAPTER 2

Dylan squinted and sneezed as the grey and orange dust swirled around him, smelling of concrete. He badly wanted a swig of ginger ale. Unsure of why he wasn't dead, he turned around so the light wind was at his back, and took off his hat to wave it through the dust. As the dry cloud began to dissipate in the breeze, he saw an animal standing in front of him.

It was about the size of a chimpanzee. The animal most closely resembled a turtle, if a turtle was capable of standing on its hind legs. It was mostly brown, and had furry skin in front where a turtle's breast shell would be. Below that, short legs and feet in the same brown fur.

Its back was not as rigid as a turtle's shell, but shaped much like one. In contrast to the breast, it was a smooth, glossy green, with swirling blue patterns that continuously moved across it. The head also was not quite as sharply shaped as a turtle, with expressive features, and particularly penetrating eyes. Perhaps its most intriguing feature was its arms. The arms appeared exactly like seal flippers made of pink putty, and they were clearly capable of amazing, shape-shifting dexterity and power.

"Wow, that was close," spoke the animal.

Dylan knew he was clearly outside reality at this point.

"That's it," Dylan said, as if to himself. He plopped his hat back on his head. "I didn't wake up. I'm having a lucid dream. I've heard about these."

"Me too!" said the animal. "I've tried to train myself to have more control in my dreams, but I can never get the hang of it."

As if the animal speaking was not enough, Dylan was further disoriented by its conversational tone, and the fact that it sounded remarkably like Don Knotts. "Really?" Dylan said. "You're really going to talk to me, and tell me you have dreams."

"Why wouldn't I?"

"I know!" blurted Dylan, having a realization. "I ate something. Something really bad. Yeah, this is a trick! Somebody put acid in my coffee or something. I get it."

Dylan heard a low hum, building slightly in volume. He looked up, and the puffy clouds in a large area of the sky looked wavy, like heat distortion.

The animal spoke again. "Hang on a sec." He quickly raised one of his pink putty arms and it extended above Dylan and flattened out like an umbrella. The hum got much louder, and there was a massive flash of light around the pink umbrella.

Dylan was still in total denial. "Cool," he said.

"Look," said the animal, "not that I couldn't keep doing this, but it's distracting, and I wouldn't want to make a mistake. Can we go somewhere and talk a minute?"

"Um, sure. Why not?"

"Oh, wait." A pink arm reached up and sliced the back of Dylan's left hand.

Dylan grabbed his hand. "What the hell?" he yelled.

"I might get impatient with all this dreaming and hallucinating crap," the animal said. "I don't really have time to slowly bring you to a realization that you've almost been killed like nine times already today. Snap to it, dude. Need you focused."

"What the hell?" repeated Dylan. He peeked at the back of his hand. He thought it was cut deeper. It wasn't bleeding, but it stung. The animal had accomplished his sensory alarm.

The animal clapped his flippers and rubbed them together. "OK, then," he said, "is there any water around here?"

Whatever was creating these utterly preposterous happenings, Dylan was done playing with this animal hallucination.

"Wait—why am I talking to you?" he said. "I'm going home."

"Ooh—ooh—this is where I get a movie line," the animal gushed. He cleared his throat and lowered his voice. "If you want to stay alive, you'll keep talking to me."

"What?"

He was back to his normal voice. "No, I mean it. Walk away from me, and you won't live eighteen seconds. Stick with me, and I'll tell you why that's true."

"Ridiculous. This can't be happening," Dylan said.

"Do I need to cut your other hand?"

Dylan instinctively covered his other hand. "No, no." He was getting frustrated with the lack of reality he was dealing with, and the fact he had no clue as to why.

"But you can't be real," Dylan continued. "Why am I having a conversation with you?"

"We're wasting time," the animal said, "so I'll be blunt. It might not feel like it, but you're on a mission to save the universe. Some people don't want you to, and they're trying to kill you. I'm trying to save your life. You have nothing to lose by humoring me, and your life to lose if you don't. Frankly, it's just flat stupid not to talk to me."

Dylan let out a sigh. He didn't care for being called stupid. "Fine, I'll play along. So, you want something to drink? I know I could use one."

"Drink?"

"You asked about water," explained Dylan, looking around. It was an absent-minded gesture, as there was nothing around them except the rubble of the warehouse.

"Oh, that. No, I meant like a body of water. A lake."

"Oh. Um, no." Dylan was confused, to say the least. "We need a lake?"

"Or an ocean. Got one?"

The animal's manner continuously took Dylan by fresh surprise. "Not exactly," Dylan answered.

He shrugged. "All right, then. I wasn't going to do this just yet, but we need a moment to rest, and I know just the place. Ready?"

"For what?"

Dylan was still standing, and the animal was still next to him, but their environment had instantaneously changed in its entirety. No rubble, no street, no outdoors. They were standing in a transparent dome about forty feet in diameter and twenty feet high at the center. The floor was covered in a low-pile blue carpeting, and the enclosure was otherwise empty. There were two devices attached to the dome shining light down throughout the place, but outside the dome it was very dark.

Dylan's whole body jerked in reaction to the change, and he nearly fell over. "Oh my God!" he yelled.

"It's OK!" the animal said.

"What the hell happened? Where are we?"

"Look at me," said the animal. When he said that, Dylan realized that throughout their brief conversation so far, he had actually not looked the animal in the eye again since the first moment he saw him.

"Look at me!" the animal repeated.

Dylan looked. He immediately felt considerably calmer.

"Relax," said the animal. "You need to sit down. Think about that."

"What?" said Dylan. "Think about what?"

"Think about sitting down and relaxing," the animal said.

This was completely outrageous. Utterly, totally outrageous. Not a half hour earlier, he was closing his car door and casually contemplating a grilled hamburger. Since then he'd been accosted by a freakish, subterranean octopus, bombarded with fire bombs from space, and shot at by a cop. Now, he was standing in an empty dome with blue carpeting, having a conversation with a furry, brown turtle with shape-shifting flippers made of pink putty that had just saved him from being crushed by a collapsing building.

Perhaps more oddly than anything, he was actually inclined to go along with it at the moment. Although it made absolutely no sense that Dylan would be able to concentrate well enough to do or think anything this animal was telling him, he felt his mind move smoothly to visions of his favorite lounge chair in his house.

"Good, good," said the animal. Dylan didn't even consider how the animal could be reacting to his thoughts. "Think about sitting in that chair and how comfortable it would feel to be in it now."

Dylan began to do so. The chair appeared in the dome, right behind Dylan.

"Yes! Yes!" the animal said, clapping his flippers.

Dylan was further dumbfounded. "I...I..."

"Sit. Sit and take a breath. We'll cover everything."

As Dylan sat in the chair, more furniture appeared in the domed room. A short chair for the animal, a rectangular, wooden coffee table between them, and a floor lamp that illuminated in place of the overhead devices, making the space a little homier. A small refrigerator also appeared next to Dylan's chair, and two glasses on the table.

"Dear God!" said Dylan.

"Relax. I'll explain it all. Have a drink," said the animal.

Surreal as everything was, he couldn't deny his mouth was very dry. "Why not?" said Dylan as he reached and opened the refrigerator. There was a nice assortment of soft drinks, including his favorite ginger ale. He grabbed a bottle and swung the refrigerator door closed, then twisted the top off and took a swig.

Perhaps it was the familiar taste of the ginger ale, but Dylan suddenly switched from bewilderment to analytical mode.

"OK," Dylan started. "I have a couple of questions."

"Sure."

"Before our surroundings changed instantly and completely," said Dylan, "my first question would have been who are you. But now with a moment to think, I'm going to go with personal safety. Since you seemed to think I was going to be killed at any moment, and you clearly no longer do, I'm going to ask, where the HELL are we? And why am I safe here?"

"Fair choice," said the animal. "You were in mortal danger because there are beings who want you dead. You are safe here because those beings have a much more difficult time finding you under water. We are under a great deal of water."

"Really?" Dylan said, shifting nervously in his chair. "So, that's why you asked about a lake. Got it."

There was nothing about this that Dylan got. Still teetering on the edge of hysterics, it was nevertheless the wildly unbelievable sequence of events that was inexplicably allowing him to speak calmly. It was overcompensation for the insanity.

"So, where are we, Pacific Ocean?" he said.

"Well, not exactly," the animal answered. "We're kind of a trillion light years from the Pacific Ocean."

"Yeah, right."

"Hey, you asked."

Dylan sipped his ginger ale. "Fine," he said, "I'll play along again. In the blink of an eye, we traveled a trillion light years to a glass bubble under water, where furniture and drinks appear out of thin air."

"Don't be silly," the animal replied. "Glass would never

hold up under this kind of pressure."

"No, of course not," Dylan said, now a trifle irritated by the absurdity of the animal's conversation. "But why here? Wasn't there someplace closer, say a hundred million light years from Earth, that was just as good?"

"I suppose there were places that would have worked, but this is one of my favorites. There aren't as many places like this as you might think."

"Oh, I'm sure there aren't," said Dylan.

"In fact," the animal continued, "there really isn't even as much water in the universe as you might think. It's pretty rare. Sure, Earth has a bunch, but I can't think of more than, say, seventy billion planets like that. Anywhere."

"Right." Dylan was tiring of this quickly, and changed the subject. "So, how about you? What sort of drunken pink elephant imagining are you?"

"Freddie," the animal said. "Call me Freddie."

"I can do that," Dylan said. "I can call you Freddie. If that's your name, that is. Wouldn't want to be calling you something that wasn't your name. You're Freddie?"

"Oh, my," Freddie sighed. "It isn't actually my name. It's just what I was suggesting you should call me. You couldn't possibly pronounce my name."

"Go ahead. Try me. Oh, wait, I know. Rumpelstiltskin."

"No, no," Freddie said. "Don't misunderstand. I'm not being dismissive or anything. I really mean you can't pronounce it, as in it would be physically impossible. And if I spoke it for you, you wouldn't hear it properly."

"Oh, admit it," Dylan joked. "It's Sue. You're an alien named Sue, and you're too embarrassed."

"Hey! I know that song," Freddie said, "but you're quite wrong, I'm afraid. What I mean is that you exist in four dimensions, and my name requires seven to be spoken."

Dylan chuckled. This just got better and better. "Really! Seven dimensions just to say your name."

"Yup. So, if I spoke it, you would only hear the really

weird parts that would exist in your four dimensions."

"OK, now why would I believe anything you're telling me if you don't even know how many dimensions we're in? This is the world of three, if I'm not mistaken."

"But you are," said Freddie. "Mistaken, that is. Time is a dimension. You exist in your three physical dimensions, as affected by time."

"Ah," Dylan said, nodding. "And you exist in seven."

"Twelve."

Dylan's eyes got big. "Twelve?"

"Yes, but my name only requires seven to be spoken correctly."

This was all just crazy ridiculous. "I see," said Dylan. "Your name needs seven, you need twelve. Exactly how many dimensions are there, if I may ask?"

Freddie's voice got all mysterious. "Nobody knows. At least thirteen. There's talk of fourteen."

Dylan mimicked Freddie's mysterious tone. "That's a lot of dimensions," he said.

"I know! Your theoretical physicists are going on about nine, or ten, or eleven, or ten-plus-one and all that, but they're way off."

"And how do you know that?"

"I'm a twelve-dimensional being."

Dylan slapped his knee. "Oh, right."

"I've met some beings from the thirteenth dimension. Those guys are weird."

"Why does that not surprise me?"

"They're dangerous, too," Freddie warned. "Very powerful."

Dylan paused a moment to consider things, and took another gulp of his ginger ale. This experience was utterly preposterous, but was at least managing to become entertaining. Accepted at face value, he was somewhere ten times as far away from Earth as he would have thought possible, sitting in his favorite chair, drinking ginger ale and listening to Freddie, the twelve-dimensional, pink-flippered, Barney Fife turtle.

None of this was even remotely possible, but Dylan couldn't figure out a way to snap himself out of whatever hallucination he was in, so he kept the conversation going until he could find the trigger that would yank him back to the real world.

"Can I ask a question?" Dylan said.

"Fire away," said Freddie.

"Why a trillion light years? Why not ninety-nine quadrillion? Come on, if you're going to make something up, make it believable. I've read a little astrophysics. The known universe is less than a hundred billion light years across, so we can't be a trillion light years away."

"I'm sorry," said Freddie, "what was that?"

"I said the known universe is only—"

"Stop. The what?"

"The known universe."

"Known by whom, may I ask?"

"Well, by Earth. By…earthlings."

"AAhhhhh," said Freddie. "And tell me, Mr. Astrophysicist, in this 'known universe,' or 'observable universe,' is the Earth at the center?"

Dylan began to realize where this was going. "Um, yes."

Freddie was playing it as somewhat of a smarty-pants at this point. "Now. Let's tap into that quality engineer head of yours, shall we? You deal in probabilities, yes? Statistical probabilities?"

"Yes."

"Good. Imagine that there is, in fact, a finite, spherical universe a hundred billion light years across. Billions and billions—oh, wait." Freddie repeated the phrase in a Carl Sagan imitation, which, of course, actually sounded like Don Knotts doing a Carl Sagan imitation. "Billions and billions of stars and planets—always wanted to do that—and among those, Earth. What are the odds, Mr. QE, what is the statistical probability of the Earth, with all its knowing earthlings, being precisely at the center of it?"

Dylan didn't answer.

"HMMMMMMMM?"

"All right," Dylan said. "Almost zero. Point taken."

"And, as I'm sure you remember from your astrophysical readings, the only reason your precious little 'observable universe' is not larger is that objects past the edge of it are moving away from you faster than the light can travel back to you, so you can never see them."

"Yes."

"So think of your observable universe as an illuminated beach ball, with ten more beach balls lying side by side. Nobody inside any of the beach balls can see the other balls, because the light from each ball can't reach the others, but that doesn't mean they aren't there.

"Now—think of the entire beach full of thousands of beach balls piled up high—each one a 'universe'—and you start to get a sense of how big the universe *really* is. All you and I did was move from one beach ball to another one ten balls away, within a universe containing countless beach balls. It's a spit, really."

"OK," said Dylan, "but there's just one little thing."

"Shoot."

"You said 'all you and I did.' OK, coupla things. First of all, 'you and I' did nothing, because I did nothing. Whatever doing was done, you did it. Second, you say that like you just slid a checker across a trillion-light-year checkerboard. Things don't move ten *inches* instantaneously, let alone ten universes."

"It's an interdimensional thing," said Freddie. "You might understand a little better after a while."

Dylan was taken aback by that casual remark. "A while of *what*?"

Freddie ignored the question. "Or, you might at least get used to it. Either way, I can't really explain it in any detail, because you're stuck in your four dimensions. Kind of.

Anyway, we've been here about as long as it's safe. Ready?"

Dylan fell on his back in a cloud of red dust kicked up from the dirt he landed in. He'd been in his chair, and there was no chair where he was now, so he fell. He also immediately noticed that there was an apparatus on his face, holding a mask over his nose and mouth, with straps around his head to keep it in place. He reached up to it.

"Don't touch that!" yelled Freddie.

"What the hell?" said Dylan behind the mask. It restricted his jaw movement a little, and the sound was muffled, but he could speak and be heard.

"You need that to breathe," Freddie instructed as Dylan began to work his way to his feet. "Don't take it off for more than a few seconds at a time. The atmospheric pressure here is OK for you, but the mix of gases definitely is not."

Dylan was standing, and looked around. Freddie had slid the checker piece again, and there was obviously no telling where or on what planet they were. Not to Dylan, anyway. Their current environment could not have been much more different than an underwater dome.

To his right was open landscape. It looked dry. There were short rolling hills with lots of light brown and red dirt, scattered rocks, and brilliant blue flowers on very short plants dotting the terrain. Off to his left, a group of small buildings that suggested a village of some kind. They looked like adobe, with very simple box construction.

"Can't stay," said Freddie. "This world will be tough on you, but it's murder on me. Read the paper in your pocket. Bye!"

With that, he vanished.

# CHAPTER 3

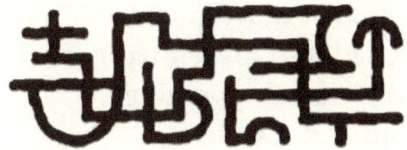

The expanse of dry dirt and desolation in front of Dylan quickly filled him with a sense of nervous fear.

"Hey!" he shouted. "Freddie!" Even though there was no one to hear, it struck Dylan that the yelling had even less inherent dramatic impact with the mask over his face.

Freddie did not appear. This situation was beyond absurd. He was abandoned in an environment so foreign he couldn't even breathe the atmosphere. He had no options whatsoever. He couldn't wake up. He couldn't go home. The only link he had in his brain to anything normal was Freddie, and since Freddie was an alien he met fifteen minutes ago, that was saying something.

Dylan was suddenly thirsty. He looked down, and saw a bottle of water in the dirt. Cool. He picked it up and examined it carefully. It was a brand he recognized, so either his fantasy was mixing alien worlds with Earth products, or Freddie brought it with them. He twisted the cap off, lifted the mask, and took a sip, without breathing. It was no ginger ale, but it was refreshing enough. Tasted like water, at least, and not some cruel hoax. He let the mask back down onto his face and put the top on the bottle.

He looked around at the bleak landscape, very happy he still had his hat in the blazing sun. He was completely at a loss for what to do. Even starting to walk had no purpose, since he had no idea where he was or where he would be walking, or even if the ground was safe. It looked it, but that didn't mean much. He did remember Freddie mentioning a paper, and he reached into his left pants pocket. Sure enough, there was a folded piece of paper there.

He pulled it out and read it.

Dylan—I know I told you this, but don't take your mask off without holding your breath. Ever. You could survive a few seconds, but it's better if you just don't risk it. And don't eat or drink anything here. Bad news. Drink your water if you get thirsty, and if it runs out, deal with the thirst. If you give in and drink something here, you'll live, but you might wish you hadn't.

Why did I bring you here? There's something here you need; I'll explain later. It's a substance called unlo. You won't find it where you are by the village, but someone in the village knows how to help you find it. Go into the village and find a building with symbols on it that look kind of like Greek letters.

That's a restaurant. Go inside and ask someone for Dillon. He has something for you. Don't mention the unlo. Just get what he has. Good luck!
Freddie

*What the bloody hell is this crap?*

"Freddie!" Dylan yelled into his mask again, hoping he could somehow call him forth. It didn't work.

At least he had something to do, if he wanted. And he

knew where the bottle of water came from.

Dylan stood and stared across the bleak, dusty landscape, trying to think back to everything he and Freddie had talked about, wondering if any of it could give him a clue what to do. He had the instructions on the note, but he was in no hurry to start on anything before collecting his thoughts.

Back before all the chit-chat about the universe and dimensions, back on Earth, Freddie told Dylan he was on a mission, that people were trying to kill him. Nobody around here. No fire balls raining down. Who knows if Freddie was telling the truth, or even knew the truth. Regardless, his options were either to strike out into the wilderness and take his chances, or go into the village like it said in the note.

Whatever this environment was, it was intensely real. Dylan was unwilling to risk an assumption that he was imagining all of it, to where he might, for instance, take off the mask. That seemed foolhardy. He decided it was a little early in this looking-glass adventure to decide he needed to strike out on his own.

He began walking toward the buildings, thinking Freddie was completely crackers. Dylan seemed to be more or less at the mercy of the brown, fuzzy turtle, but the turtle was stark-raving mad. And, to appearances, he had the power to sling Dylan around the universe at will. Yes, better do what the turtle says, for the moment.

After just a few steps, Dylan was beginning to get warm, and realized he'd been so distracted by everything he forgot he was wearing his jacket. He took the jacket off, put his water bottle in one of the jacket pockets, and continued.

He got into the village without seeing another living thing, except a few of the blue flowers, if those were alive the same way flowers were on Earth. The village was laid out just like a similar village back home would be: a single street with the buildings on either side. They looked like baked mud with a few small windows in each side, and they were all basic rectangular boxes—slightly different shapes between them, and slight variations on a cream/grey color, but all very similar and devoid of architectural style.

Dylan strolled between them, wondering how a restaurant could be functioning in a ghost town like this. The whole scenario was so outrageous Dylan likened it to being in a movie, wandering into the deserted western town like a badass marshal.

There were symbols painted on the fronts of several buildings, but they were starkly different from each other, and none were reminiscent of Greek letters. Then he saw them. He recognized immediately the characters Freddie was talking about, and the feeling that came over him was reminiscent of finding a prize in a computer video game. He wanted to click on the door.

Part of him was very scared to go inside. A lot of him, actually. But part of him was also still in firm denial that this was real. What did it matter if he plowed headlong through this dream without a care?

He stood in the quiet, dusty street, weighing his options and concluding that he had no idea how to even weigh his options. Any choice could have the same potential for danger or success, whatever that was. With that realization, carefree denial got the upper hand.

The door was the same baked mud as the walls. It looked as if they had made the whole box and then cut the door out of one side. Whatever this stuff was, it seemed to be their only construction material. The weathered brown metal handle was large and round.

Dylan grabbed it and pulled the door open, and was immediately bombarded with sights and sounds. Strange music was blaring, creatures were everywhere, trays and plates of food and beverages being swept through the air. It so startled him that he backed out and closed the door.

He turned around and looked at the deserted street.

Nope—nobody around at all.

He turned again and went inside.

The layout actually was a lot like a restaurant he might recognize, with seating tables and stand-up tables situated throughout the place, occupied by a startling collection of customers. They were mostly greenish brown, scaly, muscular, and large. Some were a shiny reddish color, some almost yellow, but just as muscular and large. All were yelling, grunting, and slopping through their food, which was clearly a variety of animal flesh of some kinds, either rare or raw. Dylan saw platters go by with the most disgusting and foul-smelling organs, garnished with one of the blue flowers he'd seen outside. It struck him as out of place.

Through the cacophony, Dylan saw a counter in the back with one of the greenish creatures standing behind it. Asking the creature about Dillon, according to Freddie's instructions, seemed like the next thing to do. By the time these few moments of reaction and thought had passed, the place was quickly quieting down as everyone noticed Dylan was there. Seems outsiders did not frequent this place.

The stares did not appear angry, at least not yet. Just curious. Dylan decided the longer this went on, the more uncomfortable it was likely to get, so he slowly began to make his way in between tables to the counter. As he did so, the place came to a virtual standstill. As he had no idea what he was doing there or why, he figured he now might as well ask everyone, since they were all staring at him. He stopped in the middle of the room.

"Anybody seen Dillon?" he said loudly, trying to overcome the mask.

It wasn't until he spoke the name that it even registered with him that it was pronounced exactly like his own, and if anyone knew his name, it would sound like he was asking for himself.

No one in the place reacted in any way to his question, so he took a deep breath, lifted the mask a moment, and announced again, "Anybody seen Dillon?"

After a moment, the creature behind the counter said,

"Aren't you Dylan?"

This struck Dylan strangely on so many levels. How could the creature speak English? Of course, this hadn't occurred to him as he was asking his own question in English, but now that he was hearing it back from one of these beings, it hit him how odd it was. And how does he know my name? And what does *any* of this have to do with *anything*?

All things considered, though, there was no reason not to continue going along with the situation. Other than not wanting to breathe, eat, or drink in this environment, he had no real concept of whether or not he was in any danger. He was completely ignoring that Freddie had told him there were beings that wanted him dead, not that it would have any greater weight than anything else he was being exposed to.

He wanted to answer, but wasn't sure how to, given the confusion in names. "Well, my name is Dylan," he began, with the mask on, "but it's spelled differently. Look." He began reaching into his pocket for the paper.

"Just get over here," said the creature. He addressed the room. "I am expecting this visitor."

The din of the room's normal activity ramped slowly back up, and Dylan began making his way to the counter again. The creature's comment was apparently sufficient for everyone to believe things were more or less normal.

"Is your name Dylan or isn't it?" asked the creature as Dylan reached the counter.

"Yes, but look—"

"I have something for you," the creature said.

"Excuse me? Are you Dillon?"

The creature looked at him intently. "You are strange. My name is Kofklapanvik."

Dylan didn't get it. "Then…why do you have something for me?"

"Because the landok left it with me."

"Um, the landok?"

The creature seemed skeptical, as if maybe Dylan was the

wrong person. "Do you not know the landok? Short, with brown front, green back, pink flippers?"

Dylan noted that he now knew what species Freddie was. A landok. "Well, yes," said Dylan, "he sent me here. Freddie."

"Ah," the creature responded, appearing more comfortable with this again. "Wait here."

Dylan stood at the counter, looking discretely around the place while the creature stepped into the back of the restaurant. The clientele was no longer paying him a lot of attention. Considering this situation a moment, Dylan realized why Freddie said to ask for Dillon. It was recognizable, easy to remember, and easy to pronounce, and it would get the job done, since the creature was obviously told someone named Dylan would be coming. Telling Dylan to ask for the creature's real name could have introduced mistakes. Dylan imagined that mistakes could be bad, though he had no way of knowing how bad.

Kofklapanvik returned from the back. "I found it," he said.

"You found it?" Dylan asked. "Weren't you waiting for me?"

"Yes," Kofklapanvik said. "For forty-two years."

"What?"

"Freddie gave me this forty-two years ago, said you would come."

"Wow. Really? How could he have known that?" Dylan said.

"From the Ancient Guard, by expectations."

"The what?"

"The Ancient Guard," said Kofklapanvik. Dylan did not react. "Do you possibly not know of the Ancient Guard?"

"Um, possibly." Dylan could tell he didn't want to explore that much further. "But never mind that. Why did you save it for this long?"

"If you never came," explained Kofklapanvik, "I would

be happy. It would mean no one ever needed it. But if you did come, it would be far too important to ever lose it."

This sounded ominous to Dylan. He still had no idea what to make of everything. He was reminded of the movie feeling again, but this time it was like he was thrown into one where everyone but him knows what's going on.

"So, what is it?" asked Dylan.

"It is the Call of the Barbadan," said Kofklapanvik.

"Say that again?" said Dylan.

"The Call of the Barbadan. Step through this room to the hallway and go out the back door. There you will see animals lashed to a post. One of them wears a saddle with 'Kof' on the side. Unlash that one and ride it away from the star."

"What does that mean?" Dylan asked.

"Keep the star to your back and your shadow in front of you." Kof pointed to one end of the object in his hand, a fanciful item looking vaguely like a nautilus shell made of mother of pearl. It was beautiful. "When you get to where the dirt turns green," Kof continued, "blow into this. Then wait."

"Wait for what?"

Kof looked at him with confusion. "How should I know?"

"All right, fine," said Dylan. "I just thought, since you had it…"

"No one has used this in thousands of years. We thought it was only a legend until Freddie brought it to me. Nobody knows what it does."

"Um, then why doesn't one of you take it out there and blow it?" asked Dylan.

"The legend," said Kof. "If any of us do it, the planet dies."

"Oh. OK. You better not do it, then."

Kof was stern. "Do not take this lightly. You save your own planet as well as ours."

*What in the world is going on? I'm not saving any planets. I'm doing what Freddie wrote on the paper, and that only because I have nothing else to do and don't know what happens if Freddie gets pissed at me.*

"All right. Take it easy. I'll do it," said Dylan, also uncertain of what happens if Kof gets pissed at him.

"Good. Do not fail." Kof held out the shell. "Burba kikik."

*What is that about?*

The last phrase sounded familiar to Dylan, but he couldn't place it. This little adventure held no end of surprises, and Dylan had a suspicion that it was only beginning.

Dylan took the shell and made his way to the back of the restaurant. He took a breath and pushed the door open. It was a lot like it had been outside the front door—dusty dirt and sun.

Just as Kof said, there was a hitching post with four animals hitched. They looked like what one might expect an armadillo might if it had much longer legs and neck. All four were saddled and bridled, though the saddles were not as elaborate as an American horse saddle. There was a seat, and a horn, and stirrups. From there, they varied between the animals as to accessories.

Dylan looked at a couple of them, and saw one with "Kof" on the edge of the saddle seat. Kof's animal had a pair of simple, burlap-type bags hanging on either side of the animal from the back edge of the saddle seat. He looked in one of them and saw a few tools and a folded piece of cloth. There was room in it, so he put the shell and his water in it. He went around to the other one, and it was almost empty save for what looked like a pistol. He stuffed his jacket in that one, wondering what sort of life Kof led on this planet where he worked in a restaurant and had a pistol in his saddlebag.

He went to the front of the animal and was about to undo the reins from the hitching post when he thought he might better take a look in this animal's face and see what was there.

He laid a hand on its grey neck, and the animal looked at him. It seemed agreeable.

"Hi. I'm Dylan. Sorry about the mask." The animal moved its head up and down, but it seemed coincidental with whatever movements the animal would normally make, as opposed to an acknowledgement of his greeting.

"We're going for a ride," Dylan continued. "We're going to go to where the dirt turns green, and call a Barbadan, whatever that is. You with me?"

The animal vaguely nodded again, but still in a way that couldn't be considered a response. Dylan chuckled. "Cool."

He unwrapped the reins from the post, then pulled them back with him as he got a foot in a stirrup and got himself slung onto the animal's back. He had only ridden a horse once in his life, on a controlled horseback ride, but he remembered the simplest things about it, which were all you were taught on a one-hour horseback ride. He had no reason to believe any of that would apply here, but also had nothing else to try.

He pulled on the reins and gave the animal's sides a gentle kick. Nothing. The animal did have armor on its back and sides, and Dylan was neither as large nor as muscular as Kof. He kicked harder. The animal moved backward, out from between the others, as Dylan swayed left and right with its movements. He pulled the reins to the right to point the animal out away from the sun, and gave another kick, making clicking noises with his tongue in classic horse-spurring fashion.

The animal started forward, with a steady walking gait. Dylan smiled. The animal walked faster than Dylan could, and in just a couple of minutes they were past the edge of the cluster of buildings and into the open terrain.

The only clue Dylan had about where to go was "away from the star," so he made sure his shadow was cast directly forward as he and his steed walked across the bright desert dirt.

The ride gave Dylan some time to think about what was going on, but it was all about questions. How could all this be real? How could all this be happening in the universe without humans knowing anything about it?

How could there be thirteen dimensions, and beings that exist in all thirteen, and how could people or things be transported across a trillion light years in an instant? How could a trillion light years even exist?

At the same time, if all those things were real, why would humans have needed to be exposed to any of it? What kind of arrogance does it take to think that humans would be included in any other goings-on in the universe? Why wouldn't any of this really happen, just because our puny three—or four—dimensions include human beings that think they have the answers?

If there really is more to the universe than humans on Earth, why wouldn't this be it?

Dylan kept riding and kept calibrating his shadow. After about an hour, there was no change in the terrain. The dirt was not turning green. He had taken several sips from his water, and was becoming concerned that he would run out before he got where he was going.

Another thing he noticed was that the sun seemed to be at the same height in the sky as it was before. There was no growth or shrinkage in the apparent length of his shadow. He wasn't sure how that could be, unless the planet's rotation was so incredibly slow as to be synchronous with its orbit around the star.

He pulled up slightly on the reins, and the animal stopped. He got himself turned in the saddle enough to look behind and see where they'd been. A lot of the ground was hard dirt, but enough was soft that he could see areas where they left tracks. There were low hills that prevented him from seeing a long way, but they had been downhill for long enough that Dylan could detect a slight curve in their tracks. Dylan had to think a couple of minutes about how that could happen, then he pieced it all together.

This was a place where the sun never sets.

Not at this time of year, anyway. He must be near one of the planet's poles, where the sun made continuous circles in the sky. That would mean for much of the year, it was continuously dark and cold here, as the other pole would have to be right now. Kof and his friends would go through at least half the year without sun, unless they migrated with it. Maybe that was it. They must relocate with the sun. How could you exist in continuous dark for half the year? Or maybe they were hibernators. Sure. They went into stasis until the sun came back.

Whatever the answer, what it meant at this moment was that by following his shadow Dylan was traveling in a huge circle. How huge it was impossible to say, but Kof telling him to travel away from the star didn't make any sense.

At that moment, Dylan was distracted by a noise above him. He looked up and saw a shiny reflection. It came closer, and the noise got louder. For a split second, Dylan thought it might be something else attacking him, but it wasn't approaching as fast as the lightning balls on the road to the electronics plant. He decided to wait and see what it was.

It was a space ship. An enormous one at that. It was a slightly flattened cylinder with rounded ends, probably three hundred feet long, sleek and silvery, with windows spaced in rows along the sides. It descended at a steady pace, in a trajectory to land about two hundred feet from Dylan. As it approached, landing gear protruded from the bottom, and the noise continued to get progressively louder. It was very loud, but not deafening.

Dylan's mount began to fidget. "Calm down, boy," he said, patting the animal's neck. "It's all right." That actually seemed to help some.

The space ship touched the ground, the legs making deep impressions in the dirt. As soon as it was settled in place, a door cracked open, hinged on the bottom so it swung down to make a ramp when fully extended.

Over the din of the space ship engines, Dylan heard a voice. "Dylan! Come quickly!" Someone was coming down the ramp. It was Freddie. "Dylan!" he yelled. "Come now! They know you're here!"

# CHAPTER 4

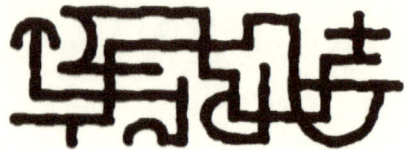

Freddie was frantically waving pink flippers as he scurried down the ramp of the ship that had landed a couple hundred feet away from Dylan.

"They'll kill you if they find you!" said Freddie. "Get up here!"

Dylan wasn't sure if there was such a thing as a gallop in the animal he was riding, but he pointed it toward the spaceship ramp and gave a mighty kick. Not only was there a gallop, it was faster and smoother than the horse he rode. In a few seconds, the two of them were skidding up the ramp into the ship, and the door began to close immediately. It latched, and before Dylan could even dismount, he could feel the ship lurch into the sky.

From atop his mount, Dylan looked around quickly. He was in what seemed to be a loading dock area, a twenty-foot square with a twelve-foot ceiling. The floor and walls were brown up to waist-high, beige above that, and they all looked like plastic. It was brightly lit, but not irritatingly so. Near several connecting corridor openings were control panels of some kind on the walls. It was a space ship, all right.

Freddie was there with four other beings, all alike but not like Freddie. These creatures had four legs for walking but a torso and two arms for doing everything else. They were similar to a Centaur, only not a horse's body or legs. More like a lion's, and the coloration and fur extended up the torso. They were large creatures, taller and heftier than the animal Dylan was riding. Their arms had hands with opposable thumbs, while the feet were paws, with claws at least as nasty as a lion's. There was no tail. The head and face were the least like a lion; they were not catlike at all. While covered with short fur, they were not too different from humans, though with a taller cranium and larger, black eyes. All in all, they were beautiful.

For lack of any precedent for anything that was happening, Dylan took his current situation as safe, based on Freddie's presence and actions.

"What the hell was all that about?" said Dylan as he swung his leg around the back of the saddle and dismounted. "Some mission this is. What did that accomplish?"

"Certainly not everything we hoped, as you ran out of time," said Freddie, "but certainly not nothing, either. You have the Call of the Barbadan?"

Looking at Freddie, Dylan pointed at his mask.

"It's OK," Freddie said. "The air is good, and we're among friends."

Dylan took off his hat and hung it on the saddle horn, then pulled the mask contraption up over the top of his head and stuffed it in the burlap bag his jacket was in.

"The shell thing," said Dylan. "Yes, I have that."

"Then the trip was not wasted," Freddie said.

Still standing next to his mount, Dylan patted its neck and said, "Well done," as he noticed in these first moments without wearing the mask that there was a musky odor about the animal. It nodded again in the same indistinct way it had behind the restaurant.

"Before I start screaming at you and all that," Dylan said

to Freddie, "do you know what this animal is?"

"Sure," Freddie said. "It's a parmalon. Wonderful beasts."

"He's been good so far. I like him. I'm sure he's thirsty as all get out."

Even as one of the four furry beings was leading the parmalon away, Freddie said, "Don't worry. The crew will take excellent care of him."

"Speaking of the crew," said Dylan, "Introductions?"

Dylan had turned a corner in his mind. Somewhere in the time alone in the desert his perception of all that was unfolding had shifted from incredulous denial to collective acceptance. He didn't know anything about anything in this absurd reality, but he had subconsciously decided to play it all as if he were in an improvisational movie. Treat everything as reality, every situation as essentially commonplace. Don't immerse yourself so far that you don't ask questions or attempt to understand, but don't remove yourself so far that you're too overwhelmed to function.

One of the beings extended a furry hand. "I am the leader of this ship. I am Urbor. I and the others in my crew are a species known as lenther."

"My pleasure," said Dylan, grasping Urbor's hand and shaking it like a human handshake, as he had no concept of anything else to do with it. The inside of Urbor's hand was skin, but the back was coarse fur, and it felt odd to grab like that, but Dylan didn't let it affect him. "I am Dylan, and I am a human. Have you met a human before?"

"I have not," said Urbor, casually releasing his grip. Apparently, the human-style handshake was normal enough. "Have you met a lenther?"

"No," Dylan replied, "and I would venture a guess that no one else on my planet has, either."

"Then we are making history. Come have a drink with me."

Dylan looked at Freddie. He said quietly, "OK to eat and

drink here?"

"You bet," said Freddie. "Excellent vittles on a lenther ship."

The other two lenthers who were there at the dock door went off down a corridor, and Urbor, Freddie, and Dylan began walking the other direction, Urbor leading the way. The dock door area felt spacious, and now they were entering a corridor not much taller than Urbor, who was about eight inches taller than Dylan. Dylan hadn't seen Freddie walk before this. There was a bit of waddle to his gait, but he was quick.

"So Freddie," Dylan said, "Obviously, I didn't get the stuff."

"The unlo? I know. There was no way to know how much time it would take. We'll have to come back."

"What is it for? Why did you say I need it?"

"We'll get to that," said Freddie.

"Who is Kof? Why did he tell me to go around in circles?"

"We'll get to that, too," said Freddie.

"Why is everyone speaking English?"

"Just relax, Dylan," Freddie chided. "Yes, there's a lot to cover, but let's get to Urbor's chamber and sit down for a minute."

They continued down the corridor. What they were walking on was more of the plastic flooring, but it was slightly padded to feel less jarring than walking on, say, concrete. Like the dock, the corridor walls were two-tone, brown from the waist down and beige on top. There were periodic lighting panels above and occasional connecting corridor openings. It reminded Dylan of a sort of futuristic hospital.

They got to a closed door on the right. Urbor opened it and they stepped inside. This was Urbor's diplomatic receiving room, and it did not look like a hospital. It was a little more dimly lit, and the general décor was darker and homier, with carpeting, a wood—or something like it—dining or meeting table, artistic decorations, a couple of sculptures, and a variety of types of furniture, for various species. The lenthers themselves sat on the floor, but many of their guests did not.

Urbor pulled a chair to the table, and gestured. "Be seated."

"Certainly," said Dylan as he rested into the chair. A chair for Freddie was also there. Urbor stepped over to a wet bar with a myriad of vessels and imbibements.

"As the first of your species," Urbor said to Dylan, "perhaps you would wish to select a suitable beverage."

Dylan rose and walked to the bar. Urbor had four decanters of liquid, and he removed the lids from each. "Some of these are definitely an acquired taste," he said. "You may wish to smell them and see if something seems pleasing."

Dylan bent over and took a whiff of the first decanter. It was terribly pungent, and Dylan bolted upright. "My goodness," he said. Urbor chuckled. "If that's an acquired taste," continued Dylan, "I don't think I've acquired it just yet."

He gave the second decanter a petulant sniff, but that was more pleasant. The third was quite inviting, a mix of nut with a hint of fruit, and definitely alcoholic. The fourth was more toward meat. A fine meal, a less appetizing drink.

"That one," Dylan said, pointing to the third.

"Excellent," said Urbor. He poured the decanter into several glasses, and brought them to the table, where all three were then seated. Urbor lifted his glass. "We share in the honor of the first meeting of lenther and human," he said.

Picking up on it as best he could, Dylan raised his glass and replied, "We share in that honor."

Urbor smiled. "Well said."

It fascinated Dylan that something like sharing a drink, with the lenther version of a toast, was a common kind of ceremonial action across whatever portion of the universe he traveled across to get where they were. It also surprised him that this situation gave him such a sense of satisfaction in himself as a representative of the human race, scoring brownie points with an extraterrestrial species this way.

Freddie didn't really count. Freddie sort of horned in and took over. Thankfully so, if people were trying to kill Dylan, but Freddie clearly didn't stand on ceremony, and Urbor did, to a certain degree. Kof didn't really count, either. The situation was too weird to call it an introduction of species. Dylan couldn't explain why this was so different; it just felt good. Maybe because Urbor made him feel like a citizen of the universe, and the other situations made him feel more like a victim of it.

He tasted the liquid in his glass. It was outstanding. Smooth, flavorful, and powerful. "My, my, my. That is just fabulous," said Dylan.

"We call it millis," said Urbor. "Of course, there are different, shall we say, grades of millis. This is one of the better ones."

"He's being modest," Freddie said. "This is the best millis anywhere. I've had a few. So has Urbor. This is from Andalatar, and it is unmatched." He turned his attention to Urbor. "It's also new, isn't it? I thought your last batch ran out."

"It did," said Urbor. "I was quite lucky to come onto another one so quickly." He looked at Dylan. "Millis is common. Millis this good is extremely uncommon."

Dylan put down his glass. "Oh, I wouldn't want to suck down your best stuff."

"Nonsense," said Urbor. "I wouldn't drink it every day, but if you are going to drink it, drink it right. Enjoy."

"In that case…" Dylan lifted his glass again and took a decent swig. "That is…*really* good. Thank you."

"The pleasure is mine," said Urbor.

"Now," said Dylan. "I'm curious about a few things."

Two intense red lights on either side of the room began

flashing, and a very loud siren went off.

Urbor set his glass down quickly and rose. "Excuse me," he said as he turned and left the room.

Freddie was hurrying around the table, and Dylan stood up. "Come with me," said Freddie.

He moved out of the room and Dylan followed. Not far down the corridor, there was a ramp up to the next higher level, and Freddie went that way. They went another fifty feet down the next level corridor, to double doors on the left. Freddie went through them, and Dylan continued behind him.

Through the doors was a set of black padded chairs of various sizes and designs. They were all facing the same way, toward large windows looking over what Dylan quickly assessed to be the bridge of the ship. "Sit and strap yourself in," said Freddie. Dylan quickly found a chair suited to him and did as Freddie instructed, as Freddie did the same.

Dylan hadn't wanted to be an annoyance by asking or commenting about anything that was happening, but once they were secured in their chairs, he felt OK with it. "What's going on?" he asked.

"Proximity alarm," said Freddie. "Somebody we don't like is dangerously close to us."

Dylan was clearly not well acquainted with recognizing one lenther from another, but thought he could tell that Urbor was on the bridge. "Is that Urbor near the center?" he asked.

"Yes."

The bridge had enormous curved windows in a sixty-degree arc across the front. The room was round, and there were consoles with information screens and control knobs and such around the perimeter, with another concentric ring of consoles between the outer wall and the center area. The entire room was softly carpeted, but there was a pad like a quilt covering part of the center area, apparently for Urbor to relax during quieter periods. Next to the pad was a post about two feet tall with a few small controls on it. Dylan guessed those were for Urbor to have access to.

All of the consoles, perhaps fifteen total, had lenthers at the controls, and Urbor was standing and moving around the center area, pointing and barking commands. The windows to the room Dylan and Freddie were in were not soundproof, but neither was any audio piped in. If Dylan listened closely, he could probably make out what was being said, but it was otherwise garbled speech.

Everything that was going on, including mostly the manner of Urbor's and Freddie's actions, gave Dylan the sense that this was more businesslike than paniclike, but the alarm was definitely a serious concern.

"Are we under attack?" asked Dylan.

"Too early to tell," said Freddie.

"Have you been through this before?"

"Yes," Freddie answered, "but not often."

The windows in the room and the bridge were positioned such that Dylan could see through a good portion of the bridge windows out into space. It looked black with star speckles, the same as it would looking up at the sky on Earth. There were no other ships in his field of view.

So far, the ship was moving smoothly, as it had been since he got on board. Other than the bustle of activity on the bridge, and the lights in various locations that were still flashing red, there was nothing obviously wrong. Yet. Dylan was consumed with observation and curiosity, but also thought about this situation during these few silent moments.

"Is this because of me?" Dylan asked.

"Also too early to tell," said Freddie. "Let's hope not."

# CHAPTER 5

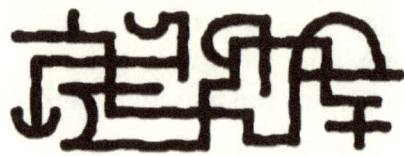

Dylan knew nothing about the greater workings of the universe or about how daily life went for Freddie or Urbor, but as he sat in his observation chair watching the bustle of activity and flashing red lights, he couldn't imagine that this was everyday stuff. And if there were really people who wanted him dead, and Freddie knew it and rescued him—at least twice now—it was very likely he was the reason for this situation.

"How could this not be because of me?" asked Dylan.

"Nobody chased us from Rondaka," Freddie said.

"Rondaka?"

"Kof's planet. Nobody chased us while we left. That means they weren't close enough yet to see this ship on our way out. That also means they'd have to independently detect you here, and that's very difficult."

"Why is that?" said Dylan.

Dylan could tell that Freddie was concerned about their situation, and he was keeping an eye on Urbor and what was going on, but he also seemed amenable to continuing to educate Dylan.

"This ship is very special," said Freddie. "It has a shell underneath the outer hull that's made of a continuous layer of two-inch-thick dallinite, one of the rarest metals in the universe. There are planets with dallinite mines where the entire mine doesn't contain as much as is in the shell of this ship."

"What does it do?"

"Basically," said Freddie, "it works like a shield, but for far more than what you think of as conventional impact weapons, or even energy weapons. It's a shield for things that happen in other dimensions."

"Such as?"

"Well," Freddie began, "for instance, we've popped around from place to place a couple of times pretty fast, right?"

"Um, yeah."

"That's because of me being in dimensions you don't exist in. But I can't do that from this ship, because of the dallinite. Dallinite is one of the elements that isn't confined to four dimensions."

"That is totally awesome," said Dylan.

"It is! It is really awesome," said Freddie, "and while it means that the beings that want you dead can't easily detect you here, it also makes the ship unbelievably valuable."

"Ah," Dylan said. "So the nasties nearby might just be marauders who've heard of this ship and are trying to steal it. Like pirates."

"Exactly!" Freddie said. "Many have tried, none successfully. Urbor is a very talented leader. He's trying to figure out what the tactical approach is."

There was an intercom system between the bridge and the observation room Dylan and Freddie were in. Urbor's voice came out of a small, round panel on the wall. "Freddie, we are going into stealth mode as a precaution. I will explain shortly."

"Stealth mode?" Dylan asked Freddie.

"Even though the ship is surrounded by dallinite," Freddie explained, "the windows can eventually allow someone to 'peek' through it. In stealth mode, dallinite panels slide across all of the windows, so the layer of dallinite is completely unbroken. We can't see, of course, but we can fly by sensors for almost everything we could need."

Even as Freddie was speaking, Dylan could see metal sheeting moving across the windows of the bridge, closing them off.

"So," Dylan said, "we're completely invisible?"

"Well, the ship isn't, but the contents are, and that's almost as good."

The doors swung open and Urbor entered. "Freddie, I am concerned."

"What's up?" said Freddie.

"Our visitors were Galderinx," said Urbor, "yet they did not attack. Not even as a ruse. They have departed."

"What does that mean?" Dylan asked.

"Regrettably, there is no sure answer, Dylan," said Urbor. "I fear that the most likely indication is that this was a scout group."

"Scouts?" said Freddie. "Galderinx don't use scouts."

"Precisely," said Urbor. "Hence my concern. If the Galderinx were here as scouts, for whom do they reconnoiter? It makes me apprehensive that our true enemies here are considerably more powerful, and may have a different agenda than the Galderinx typically display."

Freddie looked at Dylan. "He means the Galderinx are pirates, but if they're not pirating, this may be about you."

There was silence for a moment as everyone chewed on this information in their own way.

"You might be right," Freddie said to Urbor, then he turned to Dylan. "Dylan—I hate to do this, but we need to jettison."

"Jettison?" asked Dylan.

"I agree," Urbor added. "If the human separates now, it

provides the most time before the Galderinx return. We will remain in stealth mode, to travel as far as possible without Dylan on board, without anyone knowing."

"All righty, then," said Freddie. He unbuckled himself from his chair. "Dylan, time to go."

Dylan unbuckled himself also. "Go where? What are you guys talking about?"

"Urbor has a dallinite bubble pod on board," said Freddie. "You and I are going for a ride."

The three of them walked briskly down several corridors and ramps. Urbor and Freddie continued to discuss strategy and tactics, and along the way Urbor stopped at a control panel and spoke with someone in the pod room. They eventually made their way to a room very much like the dock room in which Dylan entered the ship. This one, though, had a large, round metal ball in it, sitting on a track that emerged from a tube extending into the heart of the ship.

"There we are," said Freddie.

A hatch popped open in the side of the ball, revealing an interior cavity with two seats. The crew had fitted it with chairs for human and landok while they were on their way down. It was very bare inside, except for a vent between the seats that covered the air replenishment system. Also, there was a small control panel that had a button to pop the hatch and a switch for the overhead light fixture.

"After you," said Freddie.

"You're serious?" said Dylan. "Um, this looks an awful lot like you and I are about to hurtle through space in a metal ball with no navigation capabilities, that is made of dallinite so you can't control it through your interdimensional magic."

"Bingo," Freddie said.

"Why not?" Dylan mumbled as he climbed through the hatch.

"Navigation on such a short trajectory is not necessary," said Urbor. "We are lucky enough to be able position the Zafago within only one hundred seventy-three million miles of your target planet. The time and trajectory to place you in a suitable water landing have been calculated. You are perfectly safe."

Dylan and Freddie were in their seats and harnessed. The little control panel was next to Dylan, and he flipped the light on.

Urbor grasped the hatch to close it. "Dylan, you do us tremendous honor. Burba kikik." He slammed the hatch.

Dylan wanted to know about that phrase. "Now, he's the second person to—"

The pod lurched and clanked as it retreated into the tube for jettison. It reminded Dylan of being hauled up the first hill of a roller coaster. It paused for only a few seconds, then rocketed forward and out of the ship. Once clear, there was no vibration whatsoever. They were in a vehicle with no moving parts, traversing through a vacuum.

They were quiet for a moment.

There was so much going through Dylan's mind in that moment. The launching of the pod seemed a metaphor for Dylan being fired from a cannon into this new reality. He had to keep asking himself if this could all really exist, but in spite of the apparent danger he was in, he also realized he was hoping this really was all true. At most times before Urbor's ship, he would have been thrilled to wake up from all this as a dream. Now, perhaps because the space ship made him feel more like he was in a science fiction realm he might expect, he was beginning to enjoy his introduction to the larger universe and some of the wonders it holds.

He wished he could share it with Stephanie.

His thoughts came back to where he was, and he had a lot to talk to Freddie about. He started with a light comment.

"I have a feeling this isn't the top-of-the-line escape pod," said Dylan.

"Urbor has a different one that is a miniature utility ship, with engines, navigation, the works," said Freddie. "It's just not made of dallinite. He wants to outfit the other one in dallinite, but he's not there yet."

"You have any idea how long this is going to take?" asked Dylan.

"About a half hour," Freddie answered.

"In that case, I want answers."

"Sure."

"And you're not going to interrupt and say, 'Ready?' and bop us off somewhere, because you can't, right?"

"That's right."

"OK. Now. What I started to say before was that Urbor is the second person now—maybe the third—to say that, 'burba kikik' thing to me. What is that?"

"That," said Freddie, "is a salutation of great mystical reverence and power. It comes to us all the way from the Ancient Guard."

"Aha—the Ancient Guard. Now we're getting somewhere. Kof mentioned that. What's that?"

"The Ancient Guard is a trio of very, very old and powerful beings. So old that nobody knows when they were created."

"Like God?"

"Oh, heavens no," said Freddie. "God is infinitely older than the Ancient Guard. But the Guard goes back many billions of your years."

"Cool. Burba kikik. I'll have to remember that."

"You sure will," Freddie said. "That phrase will be critical to completing your mission."

"Yeah, right, my mission," said Dylan with a chuckle. There was so much input overloading him that it was somewhat remarkable he even processed thoughts and formed words. "What is that all about?" he added. "So far, I've mostly just been running from people who want to kill me. Why is everyone treating me like I'm saving the universe?"

"Well, no pressure or anything, but you are," said Freddie. "Assuming we can keep you alive, that is."

"Um, explain."

"Ah, where to start," Freddie mused. "I am a member of a very old and dedicated group of beings called the Panel of Xarnicus. Xarnicus is one of the three beings forming the Ancient Guard. There is an object that has been in Xarnicus' care for longer than we know, at least ten billion years. It is the Holitaph. The Holitaph was created through intense mystical forces, and it has properties that surpassed even its creator's intentions. No one knows who that was. He was killed in its creation and his name was lost."

"OK, stop," said Dylan. "Already too much information."

"I'll go over it as many times as you need," said Freddie, "but you do need to get this."

Dylan could feel himself escalating quickly toward complete insanity. Romping through the universe and taking whatever comes was one thing. Even being told it was because people were trying to kill him was kind of simultaneously understood and dismissed. It was all part of that psychologically detached, improvisational movie concept he was going with.

This talk of a mission to save the universe was a little beyond the dismissable. He was no Tolkien character. He had no particular character whatsoever, in his mind, and he certainly had no use for a quest. He was a quality engineer trying to live a happy life. Saving the universe was a couple pay grades higher.

The seriousness of what Freddie was trying to explain made him remember the terror of being chased down the street being bombed by lightning balls, and feeling the car at the intersection explode. Those were like a different lifetime already, even though it had only been a few hours. If he was at work, it would just be about lunch time. Oh yeah, work. He didn't exactly get a chance to show up for the design review customer meeting.

This mission scenario was a lot; maybe too much. Dylan was having a tough time compartmentalizing it somewhere

where he could deal with it in doses. He wasn't ready to give up, but he was ready to explore the possibility.

"What happens if I quit?" asked Dylan.

"You'll be killed," said Freddie.

*OK, that was maybe a little more to the point than I needed.*

Freddie continued, "Then the Holitaph may come into the hands of creatures who could use it to rip apart the fabric of the universe. Then everyone everywhere dies. Complete annihilation of all living things, and quite a few of the nonliving things."

Dylan paused in thought.

"And then it will all be over, right?" he said.

"Well, yeah," said Freddie. "What do you mean?"

Dylan was looking down at his knee. "I mean, then nobody has to worry about anything. No worries. No fighting, no wars, nothing for anyone to get twisted about."

"True, Dylan. True. And no loving, sharing, growing," Freddie said. "Countless lives cut short before they have a chance to experience the beauty ahead of them."

Dylan had a tough time thinking about the beauty ahead of himself, in his own life. Maybe it was time to come to a realization that he'd really been in a holding pattern since Stephanie died. That he'd been emotionally unable to consider that there could be more beauty ahead of him. He'd met the love of his life, experienced that, and that was all he deserved. Thinking ahead was something that seemed disrespectful to Stephanie and the love in their relationship.

If moving on with his life was the lesson to be learned from this, it seemed awfully dramatic just for that.

"It's hard to think about that," said Dylan. "It's too big."

"No, it's not," Freddie said. "I know you lost your wife."

*How does he know about that?*

"And I know that some parts of your life have been on autopilot since then," said Freddie. "But that's exactly why you need to understand that this is not too big. It's just bigger than you've faced before.

"You can deal with this. You need to. You need to think of Earth, with billions of people, and think of each one of those people being a planet just like Earth, with its own billions of people. All of those lives need you, Dylan. Don't let those lives get cut short the way Stephanie's was. Don't shut it out. Embrace it."

"How do you know about Stephanie?" Dylan said.

"Never mind that right now. You need to rise above your urge to give up. That's not the Dylan Bruce that Stephanie loved, and it's not the Dylan she would want to see now."

His knowledge of Dylan's past notwithstanding, Freddie was certainly right about that. Stephanie would never have wanted Dylan to cling to her memory instead of living a fulfilling life. They'd even talked about it before she died. Dylan was realizing that he'd done exactly what Stephanie told him not to do. He had fallen into the safe trap of living in the past.

Dylan was quiet for a moment.

"Yeah, I guess I need to do this, huh," he said.

"I think that would be best," said Freddie. "But don't think I don't understand why you asked. I get it. I would not want to be in your shoes."

Dylan took another second to soak some of this in.

"So, not to be too obvious with the next question, but why me?"

"I suppose it might inspire you more to hear that this is your destiny or something like that," said Freddie, "but the real answer is blind luck."

"Luck?" said Dylan, thinking that wasn't exactly the word he'd use.

"Or call it chance, if 'luck' doesn't quite fit."

"What part of this was chance?" Dylan asked.

"Well, Thergon—that's the tentacled friend you encountered in the parking lot—could have met anyone. By chance, it was you."

"Chance? He wasn't there on purpose?" said Dylan.

"No," answered Freddie. "He was going...somewhere. He was dying, and his aim was a little off."

This struck Dylan as something of a revelation. He was infused with purpose. "In that case," said Dylan, "it's not chance or luck. This is destiny. He just 'happened' to end up in a parking lot on Earth and I just 'happened' to be there? I don't think so."

"As you wish."

"Oh, I know what you're thinking," said Dylan. "You're about to ask me if I think rolling a seven in a craps game is destiny. No. Well, OK, sometimes it feels like it, but no, that's not the same. I can't explain it, but sometimes there's chance, and sometimes there's destiny. And don't give me that quality engineer probability crap again. That's for defective circuit boards. This is saving the universe here. This is where it's destiny."

"Glad you feel that way," said Freddie. "Now, about the Ancient Guard."

"Wait," said Dylan.

Freddie sounded confused. "For what?"

"I don't know, just don't shift gears that fast. If we're done arguing, I need to concentrate on what you're telling me."

What Dylan needed more was a few seconds to get comfortable with the feeling that his past with Stephanie was a foundation for the rest of his life, not the substance of his entire life. It was really time to move ahead with purpose. His time with Stephanie would fortify his attitude, not be a burden on it.

"Yes, this needs your full attention," Freddie said.

"All right, go ahead."

"Wait," said Freddie. "That was arguing?"

"Not really, but whatever." Dylan was back around to being in the game, excited about this movie he was in, playing the hero. Purposeful or not, there was still an awful lot to wrap his brain around, and that was still about as real as he could process in his mind.

"So, what's this Holitaph?" said Dylan.

"OK. The Holitaph embodies tremendous power. Nobody even knows how much." Freddie made his voice low and mysterious. "Some say it taps into the fourteenth dimension."

"And that's a bad thing?" said Dylan.

"It depends," Freddie said. "Not everyone believes in the fourteenth dimension, but those that do call it the Havoc Dimension. If you can access the fourteenth dimension, you can selectively alter time in different areas of the universe."

"So?"

"Dylan, think of it. In all the dimensions we know, time affects the entire universe at once. Time is time. Imagine we're sitting in your house on Earth and there's a glass of water in front of you."

"That'd be great," said Dylan.

"Yes, but think if I could take just the glass of water and move it even one second back in time. It would be thousands of miles away from us! We're rotating on the surface of the Earth, and hurtling through space relative to the sun, and spiraling around the center of the Milky Way, and on and on. Sitting still is a deceptive illusion; you're really traveling incredibly fast all the time, relative to the rest of the universe. Someone with the power to selectively alter time for different pieces of the universe could quickly and easily destroy everything!"

"So why hasn't anybody done that yet?" asked Dylan.

"Because the Holitaph has been in the care of Xarnicus for longer than most creatures in the universe have been alive."

"And Xarnicus is one of the Ancient Guard?"

"Yes!" said Freddie. "He is one of the oldest, most powerful, and most benevolent beings that has ever existed. The Holitaph was entrusted to his care to keep it safe, and it's been so for a very long time."

"Until recently," said Dylan.

"Yup. It was stolen from him, and that is no small feat."

"Sounds like it."

"It's even harder than that."

"Right."

"I mean," said Freddie, "what I mean is it's not just that Xarnicus is powerful. The Holitaph is bonded to its owner. It's a very deep and intense bond, and no one could have stolen it without going to great lengths to break the bond. It's that bond that would allow someone with less integrity than Xarnicus to use the Holitaph recklessly, with disastrous results."

"So, why doesn't Xarnicus get it back himself, if he's so old and powerful? Isn't that what we're doing? Getting the Holitaph back for Xarnicus?"

"Well, yes," Freddie said, "but we already have it."

"Excellent!" Dylan exclaimed. "Let's take it back to Xarnicus."

"Um, it's not really that simple."

Dylan sighed. "Of course. Nothing ever is."

"It's bonded with you," said Freddie.

"What?"

"The Holitaph has been bonded to you."

"When did that happen?" said Dylan.

Then a light went on in Dylan's head.

"Oh, wait," he said, "are we talking about that black thing?"

"The black cube Thergon passed to you, yes. What'd you think we were talking about?"

Dylan was a little defensive. "I don't know. Anything. I'm under a lot of stress here." He paused in thought. "So," he continued, "this saving the universe thing isn't on me just because I was there when Thergon died. It's because he passed the black cube to me."

"Yes. He spoke, right?"

"Yeah. I think it was that burba kikik thing."

"Those words from him to you with the Holitaph in your

hand created the bond," said Freddie.

"Oh, well, then," said Dylan, "I just give the cube to somebody better at this, right? I hand it over with a 'burba kikik,' and it's a done deal. I go home?"

It was Freddie's turn to sigh. "Not really."

"Naturally."

"Once the bond is created," Freddie explained, "there are only two ways to break it."

"Yes?"

"One is the Kan Pri."

Dylan got excited. "The Grand Prix? A race?"

"Not hardly. The Kan Pri. It's a ritual. Very difficult to pull off."

"What's the other way?"

"Your death."

# CHAPTER 6

Hurtling through space inside a dimly lit metal ball, Dylan was continuing to mull over the perpetual information stream bombarding him. He was also thinking about how hungry he was. A steak and a glass of that millis stuff he had with Urbor would be welcome indeed.

The metal bubble environment itself was quite odd, because there was no noise whatsoever. Dylan and Freddie could hear each other breathe. There was also no sense of movement, including rotation, as there were no detectable gravitational fields around them yet. There was only the two of them, silence, and a slight odor like machined metal, which Dylan presumed was the pod, but could have been Freddie, for all he knew.

The situation Freddie was describing did not sound good. Freddie said a Kan Pri was difficult to pull off, but Dylan didn't really know Freddie enough to assess what that was likely to mean. All the same, one option was difficult, and the other was worse.

"So. Kan Pri or death," said Dylan. "I think I prefer the Kan Pri."

"I do, too," said Freddie.

"So, this thing is bonded with me," Dylan said. "We need to get it back to Xarnicus, then break the bond with me so it can bond with Xarnicus again."

"Very good!"

"Well, where's Xarnicus?"

Freddie began slowly. "It's not…"

"…that simple. Right," said Dylan.

"Well, I can't help it if you aren't familiar with the ins and outs of thirteen dimensions."

"Which reminds me," Dylan said. "If you're all twelve-dimensioned, how can I see you? You look pretty three-D to me."

"What you're seeing is just a three-dimensional spatial representation of me," Freddie said. "And frankly, it's pretty rare. Not many twelve-dimensioned beings can exist in three-D."

"Why not?"

"Think about it. Could you live in only two dimensions?"

"Of course not. But—"

"But nothing. Same concept. In fact, not even everyone on the Panel of Xarnicus can exist in three-D. That's one of the reasons they chose me to guard you."

"You're guarding me?" said Dylan.

"Well, what the heck else did you think I was doing?" Freddie said. "Breaking falling bricks over your head? Blocking a rahoga wave? Rescuing you with Urbor's ship in the desert? Duh."

"How am I supposed to know?" asked Dylan.

"Fine," said Freddie. "But yes, I was chosen to be your guide and guardian through this. To be honest, it's one of most honorable and exciting things I've ever done, and I've been around a while."

"Oh, yeah?"

"Not anything even approaching the Ancient Guard, but in terms of your years, about a million."

Even with everything else, this was especially outrageous. "No way!" Dylan said.

"Way."

"You're a *million* years old?"

"Give or take."

"Wow. Just wow," said Dylan. He paused. "I have some questions."

"Don't bother. I didn't start paying any attention to Earth until World War I."

"Dang."

"What can I say? It's a big universe, and I've only covered one tiny corner of it."

"What do you mean?"

"I mean there's lots more to see," said Freddie.

"You haven't been to the whole universe?" Dylan asked.

"Heavens, no. Oh, I know a lot about it, sure, but I haven't seen all that much. Do you travel?"

"More, lately."

"Very funny," Freddie said. "I mean, you live in Michigan, right?"

"Right."

"Ever been to St. Louis?"

"Yup."

"The Grand Canyon? Yellowstone?"

"Yes, both," said Dylan.

"Los Angeles?"

"No."

"Rome?"

"Nope."

"But you know things about them, yes?"

"Sure."

"So, because of everything you've heard about LA and Rome, you believe they're there and all that, but you haven't actually seen them. Same with me. I know things about most of the universe, because of all the beings I've known, but I have a lot more traveling to do."

"Have you ever met Xarnicus?" asked Dylan.

This was a bit of a sore spot. "No," Freddie said quietly.

"Why not?"

"It shouldn't bother me," said Freddie. "Most of the Panel hasn't, actually."

Dylan was sensitive to the fact that Freddie clearly wished he had stories to tell of meeting Xarnicus, but was also at a loss for understanding how the Panel operates. "What do you guys do?" he asked.

"Xarnicus and the Ancient Guard don't move around much. They stay hidden. Very few beings have seen them over the past fifty billion years. Long, long ago, the Panel of Xarnicus was formed as a society dedicated to protecting the interests of the Ancient Guard. There are three in the Ancient Guard, and we serve on behalf of all three, but we're known as the Panel of Xarnicus because he is the oldest.

"Most members of the Panel go their entire lives without having to ever act in their capacity as protectors of the Ancient Guard, but the Guard is too important to go without constant vigil. Without the Panel, there'd be no one to chase down the Holitaph, nobody who even knows what it is and what it means. No one but wreakers, that is."

"Wreakers?" said Dylan.

"The wreakers of havoc," Freddie said. "Those who disturb order, peace, and growth, for the simple, perverse pleasure of doing so."

"Had a roommate like that once," Dylan said. He wasn't joking; freshman year of college, one of his roommates was out of control with things like vandalism and other social mayhem. The roommate got expelled, and almost managed to take Dylan with him.

Dylan soaked in a little more of this for a moment. Then he said, "Can I ask another stupid astrophysics question?"

"No such thing. Fire away."

"Human models for the age of the universe are something around fourteen billion years. When you talk about the

Ancient Guard being dormant for the past fifty billion years, I presume they were active for a lot longer than that. How does that work?"

"Easy," Freddie said. "Describing it as simply as I can, your age of the universe is back to the Big Bang. That's just the most recent node in universal cycles. Ever heard of the Big Crunch?"

"I don't think so," said Dylan.

Freddie smiled. "You need some more reading, then. The Big Crunch is what came before the Big Bang, while the universe was collapsing. That was the end of a cycle, then the bang was the beginning of a new one. Just one cycle, bang to expansion to collapse to crunch, is in the neighborhood of a trillion years, and who knows how many cycles there's been. For all we know, trillions of those. Quadrillions. A googol.

"So, you need to let go of your tiny, recent concept of time just like you do your tiny, constricted idea of the edge of the universe. I'm not judging; I'm just sayin'. I bet even the Ancient Guard don't know how old they are, but even if it's five hundred billion years, that's still only half a cycle. So, at the same time it's really hard to fathom how old the Guard is, they're still just a flash in the pan. Just a speck in the timeline of the universe."

Dylan shook his head. "That just completely blows my mind."

"Yeah, it's pretty awesome to consider, eh?" said Freddie. "And you and me? So much smaller than that speck. You're, what, thirty-three? And you were freaked that I'm a million years old? Believe me, compared to the universe, we're basically the same age."

Dylan chuckled. "Yeah, I guess so."

"Now. Listen up," said Freddie, his tone becoming more serious. "Speaking of the magnitude of the space and time of the universe, here's where you should understand the magnitude of what we're doing. What I described about the power of the Holitaph?"

"Yeah," said Dylan.

"About how it could potentially tap the fourteenth dimension and result in utter chaos?"

"Yes."

"Understand what that means. Destruction of the universe. Upsetting the cyclical expansion and collapse. Don't even think of the whole idea of infinity, just think of, say, a trillion cycles of the universe, each taking a trillion years. In all that time, in all those trillion-trillion years, through all the lives of every being that has ever lived, no one has ever done what the Holitaph would let them do. In the wrong hands, it would end everything. No more bangs. No more crunches. No more lives. The end."

Dylan was quiet.

"Dylan," Freddie said, "I want you to know I really do understand if you don't want to go through all this. The burden is...well, as heavy as it could possibly be."

Dylan was still quiet.

Freddie let him think about it as long as he wanted.

Finally, Dylan said, "Let's do it."

"Oh, good," Freddie said with relief. "That's great, 'cause if you said no, I'd have to kill you right now and start down Plan B."

It didn't even register with Dylan that despite Freddie's manner, he was absolutely serious about that remark. It could have been because other possibilities were already not worth considering. Once the decision was again reinforced in his head, that meant instant and complete commitment. Dylan was now concerned only with the task at hand, disregarding everything else.

He thought some more. "So, this Thergon character had the Holitaph with him."

"Please," said Freddie. "I think you can tell I appreciate the value of flippancy in times like these, but Thergon was a very old and close friend. A member of the Panel."

"Oh. I'm so sorry," Dylan said.

"It's OK, just letting you know."

"All right," said Dylan, pausing briefly. "So he had the Holitaph, right? Why didn't he go to Xarnicus and give it back?"

"No time," Freddie replied. "Xarnicus is too difficult to get to, and Thergon was dying. He was actually just trying to hand it off to another Panel member."

"Can I ask why he was dying?"

"He had the Holitaph," said Freddie, "but he was not bonded with it. He was trying to avoid the situation we're in right now. But by not bonding with it, he was on borrowed time. The Holitaph strengthens and enhances anyone it's bonded with, but it is too powerful to be held by anyone it isn't, for too long. Thergon was liberating the Holitaph from those who stole it from Xarnicus, and was gravely injured in that fight. Between the injuries and the debilitating energy of the Holitaph, he didn't have as much time as he needed. At the last moment, he made his final move, but missed his target in the Carboram galaxy and ended up under the parking lot in Michigan."

"Wow," said Dylan.

"At that point, he couldn't risk giving it to someone it would kill," Freddie explained. "Besides all the unseemly killing of people, if it stayed unbonded on Earth it could have been lost for a long time. Beings in twelve or thirteen dimensions have ways to locate things you wouldn't understand, but the Holitaph is shielded from that." Freddie looked down. "Oh, this is so hard to explain." He sighed. "The bottom line is, no one on the Panel of Xarnicus would have been able to detect it on Earth without an old-fashioned, three-D search. Thergon had to bond it with you. So he spoke the words."

"Burba kikik."

"Yes," said Freddie. "And once you were bonded with the Holitaph, that allowed me to locate you. It was difficult, but without your bond with the Holitaph it would have been impossible. Regrettably, it also allowed those who are trying to kill you to find you, too, and here we are."

Dylan was still thinking about the curious phrase. "What exactly does 'burba kikik' mean?"

"You mean, like a translation?" Freddie said.

"Yeah."

"Oh. Well, 'burba' is similar to bestowing, but it's more than that. It's like an infusion. And 'kikik' is a word describing the combined energy of everything that exists in all thirteen dimensions. That includes lots more than it sounds. Far more than power; wisdom, communal awareness, so much more. Not all dimensions are spatial, as you know from experiencing time. So, 'kikik' is really an awesome concept. It's quite simply…everything. And 'burba kikik' then means, 'May you be indelibly infused with every single thing the universe has to offer.' It's not a casual thing. It's not 'have a nice day.' And in some circumstances, such as the passing of the unbonded Holitaph, those words carry mystical power of their own, to which the Holitaph reacts by bonding."

"It reacts?" said Dylan. "It's alive?"

"No, but nearly, in a sense," Freddie said. "You know well that inanimate materials react. They have characteristics. Put an acid and base together and watch the fun."

"Yes, that's true," Dylan said.

"The Holitaph's characteristics extend to thirteen dimensions, and it has very unique and extremely powerful qualities. So yes, it can and does react to certain words being spoken."

"Fascinating," said Dylan.

"And so much more," said Freddie.

Out of nowhere, there was a lull. It wasn't for lack of discussion material. It just happened.

Then, Dylan spoke up again. "So, tell me…"

"Yeah?" said Freddie.

"In the middle of all that, I heard you say the Holitaph enhances whoever it's bonded with."

"Sure did."

"Well? Am I enhanced?"

"Absolutely."

"I don't feel enhanced," said Dylan.

"I guess maybe you wouldn't notice yet," Freddie said, "but it will increase over time. Think back to the underwater dome we sat in."

"OK," said Dylan.

"I told you to think of your chair," said Freddie, "and it appeared, right?"

"Well, a chair appeared, exactly like the one in my house, yes."

"Trust me, it's not in your house any more." Freddie smiled and patted Dylan's knee with his flipper. "You, my friend, are in the Stream."

There was a lot of nonsensical stuff going on, but this really made absolutely no sense. "The what?" Dylan said with a sigh.

"The Stream of Consciousness," said Freddie. "It's one of the thirteen dimensions."

"Which one?"

"What do you mean, 'which one?' They're not numbered."

"No?"

"Um, no," Freddie said. "Ah, you earthlings. You think in terms of the Fourth Dimension, or maybe even the Fifth Dimension—especially in Motown—but they aren't counted. They just exist. And beings exist in dimensions that are not prerequisites for others. I know of at least three different types of eight-dimensioned beings that exist in different groups of eight dimensions. They don't progress sequentially."

"I'm not sure I follow," said Dylan.

"OK, let's say they're numbered. Dimensions one through thirteen. There are, for instance, eight-dimensioned beings that have the four you do, plus five, seven, nine, and ten. Then there are others that have your four plus five, eight, eleven, and twelve. And believe it or not, there are some that don't exist in your spatial dimensions at all."

"Cool," said Dylan.

"So it's not a matter of tacking more dimensions on to a list that everyone starts with. Any being may or may not exist in any configuration of dimensions."

"Right."

"And one of those dimensions—one very special dimension—is the Stream of Consciousness. It is one of the rarest and most amazing dimensions to exist in. It is a sort of collective awareness that certain beings all over the universe drift in and out of. And with that collective awareness comes collective abilities. Now, with your chair, I helped on that one a little, but it was basically you. I had no idea what chair you were going to think of. You brought it to the dome. Across a trillion light years. By being connected to the Stream of Consciousness."

Of all the freaky things Dylan was learning at light speed here, this was far and away the freakiest. A dimension of collective consciousness? "You have got to be kidding me," he said.

"I kid you not," said Freddie. "And it's being bonded with the Holitaph that connects you with the Stream. So I'd say yeah, you're a little bit enhanced."

"You're serious?" said Dylan. "I'm in another dimension right now?"

"Serious as a heart attack."

"How does it work again?"

"The Stream of Consciousness connects your awareness to that of a select group of species around the universe who are also in the Stream of Consciousness dimension."

"That's what I thought you said," said Dylan. "You're telling me I'm connected to living beings that right now are, like, fifty billion galaxies away from me?"

"And farther."

"That's just...weird," Dylan said. "Why don't I feel

all...I don't know, connected?"

"You will," Freddie said. "We'll try some more things. Not now. The dallinite blocks the Stream. That's why it's a good stealth barrier for the Zafago."

"The Zafago?" Dylan asked.

"Urbor's ship."

"Ah, right."

"When I described the shell acting as a shield for things in other dimensions," Freddie said, "I was talking about the Stream of Consciousness. It was the Stream that allowed both me and our enemies to locate you on Earth."

"So I've been in that dimension since Thergon gave me the Holitaph?"

"Yup. You'll get more used to using it," Freddie explained, "and once you do, it will eventually become second nature. If you get really good at it, you'll see and hear things from very far across the universe, that others in the Stream are seeing and hearing. Sometimes even their thoughts."

"I can read minds?"

"Sort of," Freddie said. "You'll see. Actually, your subconscious is reading them all the time already. You asked me once how everybody's speaking English."

"Oh, yeah! What's up with that?"

"Well," said Freddie, "with me, it's because I learned English. I know more languages than you can imagine, in lots of dimensions. With others, though, like Kof and Urbor, it's the Stream. You see, the Stream knows the minds of even people that aren't connected, like Kof. Urbor is—he's the only five-dimensional member of the Panel—but Kof isn't. But you are, so the Stream translates. Well, it doesn't do it, it...facilitates it. It provides for continuous translation of speech. As long as you're bonded with the Holitaph, you can speak with any being you encounter."

"Wow!" said Dylan.

"Couldn't agree more," said Freddie. "The Stream provides for all kinds of wondrous things. And since most of the beings in the Stream of Consciousness are also in many other dimensions you aren't, you'll be able to interface with three-D objects in a whole new way. Such as teleporting your chair. Or yourself."

"You're serious?"

"Totally, dude. Welcome to the Stream."

"That's…awesome!" said Dylan.

"I know!" echoed Freddie.

The pod clunked and lurched to one side. It took them completely by surprise, as it had not been long enough to reach their target planet yet, and it was definitely not water they hit.

"What the hell was that?" barked Dylan.

"Don't know," said Freddie.

They clanked around a couple more times, then nothing. Dylan and Freddie looked at each other, wondering where they were. There were no windows, no navigation system, no way to know what was outside, and no way to use the Stream to find out.

There was a knock. Four tings on the outside of the bubble, from something that sounded like metal, like someone was tapping on it with a tool.

"Think it's Urbor?" said Dylan.

"Nope," Freddie said. "Urbor can open this from the outside. Whoever did that is most likely not our friend."

The four taps came again, faster and harder this time.

"How long can we last in here?" Dylan asked.

"Not long enough," said Freddie, "especially since we have no idea what we're waiting for."

"Probably best to just open it and see, huh," said Dylan.

"Not yet," Freddie said, unbuckling himself. "This is not like the movies, where people take prisoners for no reason when they should just kill them instead. Make no mistake. The beings that are after you are after you to kill you. They need to break your bond with the Holitaph."

"Understood," Dylan said. He was in the game. "So,

what's the plan?"

"Get yourself unharnessed," Freddie instructed. Dylan began to do so as Freddie continued, "When you pop the hatch, we're on the attack. We can't give them a chance to fire a weapon in here, where we're sitting ducks."

"Agreed," said Dylan, "but exactly what do you propose I attack with?"

"Well, it won't be attacking so much as active defense," Freddie said. "I'll spring out first, so I can shield you. As soon as I'm outside the dallinite, I'll be able to do whatever is necessary to protect you. You come out as close behind me as you can. The moment we're both outside the bubble, I'll take us somewhere else."

"Sounds good," said Dylan. "Let me know when you're ready to spring."

"Wait," said Freddie. "I'm not so good at springing. You're better. See if you can get between the seats a little, with your legs under you, and I'll get in front of you. Hold me there, then I can push the button and you can lunge with me as a shield."

"Oh, right. I like it."

"That way," said Freddie, "we leave the bubble as closely together and as quickly as possible."

"Right."

Dylan scooted as much as he could to get between the seats, squatting with his back on the ventilation grate. As it worked out, he could only get his right leg underneath him, and his left leg had to push out over the chair he was sitting in. Freddie got situated basically sitting on Dylan's right knee. Dylan put his right arm around Freddie.

"All right," said Dylan. "I think this is as ready as it gets."

"OK," Freddie said. "Here we go."

Just as Freddie was reaching for the hatch button, the rapping came again on the outside of the pod. It was slower, and heavy. It somehow sounded angry. Dylan was thinking the timing was about as good as they could ask for; without knowing anything more than they did, it seemed the element of surprise could be best while somebody was banging on the bubble.

At the third clang, Freddie hit the button.

# CHAPTER 7

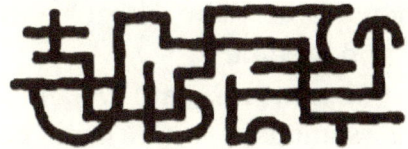

The pod hatch popped. As it flung down, Dylan sprang with all he could.

The surprise worked. Dylan couldn't see anything except a large, round pink shield in front of them, courtesy of Freddie's left flipper. For a split second, he heard a variety of sounds, like buzzing and humming, then the two of them tumbled onto the blue carpeting of the underwater dome.

Dylan was on his back, looking at Freddie, who was picking himself up and wiping his flippers in a gesture mimicking someone fixing their sleeves. "Sweet," he said.

"Are you OK?" asked Dylan.

"Sure am," Freddie answered. "You?"

"Yup."

"Good," Freddie said. "Now. We have a new problem."

"New problem? Great," said Dylan, getting to his knees. "I'm all about new problems. What's up?"

"Well, obviously, we were intercepted," said Freddie.

"Obviously." Dylan brushed his hands together and stood, looking around the dome. There wasn't much there, but everything that was before, still was. Two chairs, coffee table, lamp, refrigerator.

"That wasn't supposed to be possible," Freddie said, finding his way to his chair. "The dallinite should have prevented it, as I was explaining just a few moments ago about the Stream of Consciousness."

"Ah, right," Dylan said. "If we couldn't 'see' out, they shouldn't have known I was there, either."

"You got it," said Freddie.

"So, what does that mean?" said Dylan.

"That means someone somewhere has changed the game," Freddie said. "Someone can penetrate the properties of dallinite. There is some extremely powerful influence afoot."

Dylan thought about the new developments as he stepped over and sat in his chair. "Question about the Stream of Consciousness."

"Shoot."

"You said, what, that I brought this chair here, right?"

"Right," said Freddie.

"So, this isn't a reproduction of my chair. It's the actual chair. If I were in my house right now, the chair would be gone?"

"Yes," Freddie confirmed. "The Stream doesn't allow you to create things out of thin air."

"Then, where did all this other stuff come from?" asked Dylan.

"Oh, various places," Freddie said with a mischievous grin. "And I can send them back there any time. All right, maybe I shouldn't have borrowed them, but they'll never know. Except the pop. Whatever we drink will be permanently missing from a bottling plant in Arkansas."

Dylan chuckled. "I see. Well, that's their contribution to saving the universe, then."

Freddie also laughed lightly. "Yeah, I'd say you're entitled."

Dylan opened the refrigerator and grabbed another bottle. "Next question: if these powerful beings want me dead, why aren't they here right now? Can't they tell where I am?"

"The Stream is in constant flux," Freddie said. "I don't know why, it's just the way it works. This isn't the best analogy, but think of it like software your office has a limited pool of licenses for. When the limit of people are logged in, nobody else can until somebody logs out. It's kind of like that. So, it can take time for somebody to hone in on the awareness of somebody else in the Stream. Admittedly, it's often instantaneous, but not always."

"OK," said Dylan.

"And other things can affect it, too," Freddie continued, "like dallinite. And water. Water isn't as effective as dallinite, but it slows things down. And the fact that some beings that have been around a while and are very skilled, like myself, can keep ourselves out of it if we want. So, in this case, somebody trying to find you has to look for you while your consciousness is in the Stream, without access to me—the only other person that knows you're here—and do it through the muddiness of a water barrier. It takes some time. Lets us catch our breath."

"Right," Dylan said. "So, while we catch it, what's next? Back to Rondaka for the unlo?"

"Hey, nice memory," said Freddie. "But that might not be our best move. For starters, all your stuff, including Kof's parmalon and the Call of the Barbadan, are on Urbor's ship."

"Oh, yeah, about that," said Dylan. "What is a Barbadan, and why do I need to call it?"

"Not now," said Freddie. "We'll cover that when we're ready for you to go back. Right now we need to focus on what's next."

"Um, fine," Dylan said. "Then, what's next?"

"What's next is tracking down the Arbar."

"What?" Dylan said. "How many of these things are there?"

"OK," said Freddie. "We need the Arbar, the Studepron, and some unlo."

"Shadrach, Meshach, and Abednego?" Dylan joked.

"Cute, but no—the Arbar, the Studepron, and some unlo."

"I know about the unlo, obviously," said Dylan, "but what are the Arbar and the Studepron?"

Freddie got a pop of his own, reaching out with a pink flipper that seemed to effortlessly change shape as required to grasp the refrigerator handle, open it, reach inside while holding the door open, grab a pop, and close the door again.

Dylan wasn't sure whether to be more amazed by watching that happen or by the fact that he wasn't more freaked out by it. For the first time, it occurred to him that the Stream of Consciousness might be having some influence on his acceptance of his circumstances. That idea struck him as wickedly thrilling. He was part of something huge and vibrant and new, part of something that mattered in a way nothing ever had before.

It helped that Freddie seemed enthusiastic. It wasn't easy to get a read on him sometimes, but in general Freddie's attitude was upbeat, even flippant, and that was good. Dylan had no idea who else on the Panel of Xarnicus might have been available for Freddie's job, but he was glad they chose Freddie. As interesting as it was to meet Urbor, for instance, Dylan couldn't imagine going through all this with him. For that matter, he already couldn't imagine trying to go through this with anyone but Freddie.

Freddie adjusted himself in his chair a little, getting ready to speak. "OK. The Arbar and Studepron are artifacts from billions of years ago. They hold mystical characteristics that no other objects do."

"Wait a sec," said Dylan. "That's not the first time you've used the term 'mystical' in your comments to me. What do you mean by that. Magic? Is there a dimension of magic?"

"Not the way you're thinking," said Freddie. "But almost

anything that enters your four-dimensional reality—excuse me, five!"

Dylan had a quizzical look on his face.

"Yes, five," said Freddie. "Your three spatial dimensions, time, and now the Stream. You, my friend, are now a five-dimensioned being. In a sense, if you were to define humans as four-dimensioned, you've actually—if temporarily—become an entirely new and unique type of being!"

Dylan smiled.

"I know, it's totally awesome," Freddie continued. "Even after a million years, there are wondrous things I've never seen before, and you, my friend, are one. Not that there are no other five-dimensioned beings. There are plenty. But not that used to be human! But to get back to your question: pretty much anything beyond those five dimensions that interfaces with you is going to be perceived as supernatural. And it kind of is, actually. I mean, it's not beyond all nature, but it's beyond yours.

"I'm sure you realize that anyone from, say, the sixteenth century would think most of your technology today is magic. The same is true for you, of technologies that are hundreds of years away. But you can expand 'technology' to include all natural properties beyond the realm of your perception or understanding. Moving your chair here? Clearly magic. Unless you know about the Stream. I know you don't really understand the Stream, you just understand that it exists and that you're involved, but that's enough for you to know that it's not magic. Right?"

"Right," said Dylan.

"So the 'mystical' properties I refer to," Freddie explained, "are nothing more than properties they have because of their characteristics in a number of dimensions beyond what I can explain. I really don't mean for it to sound like I'm patronizing you. You're a smart guy. I just use a term you identify with because it's not possible for you to understand the intricacies of why they appear mystical."

"OK, that's cool," Dylan said.

"And actually, I like the term 'mystical,' because even though these properties have a natural explanation, they're still completely awesome, and incredibly old and rare, and that is what 'mystical' conveys for me. They're natural, and saying that merely means they obey the laws of nature, as everything does, but it doesn't mean they're mundane. Quite the opposite. You know your Seven Natural Wonders of the World?"

"Sure."

"Well," said Freddie, "think of these things as the Natural Wonders of the Universe. Of all thirteen dimensions of the universe, and how they interact. They provide for remarkable things, like reacting to words, like the Holitaph does when it bonds. Again—not to make you feel spoken down to or anything, but you just have to accept that you're eight dimensions short of a deck, and deal with it."

"That's OK, I get it," said Dylan. "I only have five dimensions, and I only use ten percent of my brain and all that."

"That's another thing," said Freddie. "Where on Earth did you people ever get the idea that you only use ten percent of your brain?"

"I don't know," Dylan said, "it's just like an accepted situation."

"It's hogwash," said Freddie, "and you should know that if you think about it for two seconds. How many species on your planet develop physical characteristics they don't use to survive?"

Dylan thought. "Not many."

"Less than that," said Freddie. "Near zero. Sure, there's a few things like an appendix here and there, but generally animals have what they need and use. Period. You really think humans would just randomly develop ninety percent more brain than they need? How would that even happen?"

"Yeah, I guess you're right," Dylan said.

"Trust me, Dylan, you're using your whole brain."

"Then what about differences in intelligence and all that?" Dylan asked.

"Oh, sure," said Freddie, "people use their brains more or less efficiently than each other, or may even have cells or chemical variations that change performance, but none of that has anything to do with how much brain you use as a species. If humans only used ten percent of their brains, they would only *have* ten percent of their brains. Talk about your natural laws—there's one that should have slapped a few of your scientists in the face a while back."

Dylan took a sip of pop. "Wow, how'd we get off on that?"

"Whatever—I get excited," said Freddie. "Never mind. What were we talking about?"

"Um, mystical items."

"Oh, yeah," Freddie said, standing up. "Well, now we're out of time again. Ready?"

Dylan fell on his back again, this time on thick, tropical vegetation.

"Will you stop that!" he said.

"Shhh," Freddie whispered. "Not too loud. You don't want the Tanbacks to hear you."

"The what?" Dylan asked quietly.

"Tanbacks. They might kill you, and it won't have anything to do with the Holitaph."

"What?"

"They've never seen something like you," Freddie said, "and they don't know what you taste like."

Dylan got to his feet. "Where the hell are we?"

"Balytre," said Freddie.

Of course, that meant nothing to Dylan. He looked around, but he couldn't see far. The vegetation was thick, with tall trees and lower shrubs, all with enormous leaves of different shapes. He and Freddie were in a tiny clearing with a combination of wide-bladed grass about eight inches tall, and what looked like a kind of clover. He heard sounds he instinctively interpreted as small animals in the distance, all around. The sky was blue and Freddie had not equipped him with a mask, so he took this as an atmosphere similar to Earth. The greenery had a sharp smell, just short of irritating. The sunlight was at a low angle. It seemed unlikely the sun stayed that low, the way the sun on Rondaka stayed high, or else plants this thick would have a hard time. That meant it had an overhead trajectory and it was nearly dusk.

In another moment, Dylan began to associate the sounds he was hearing with specific visual identification in his head. Some were crawling animals, some climbing, some flying. He was also more aware of other beings on this planet, including Tanbacks. They were roughly four feet tall and looked and moved a lot like apes, but with no fur. They had a tough-looking skin, green in front and, of course, tan in back. Depending on the topography, wonderful camouflage.

As this was going on in Dylan's head, he began to realize it was all because of the Stream of Consciousness. He was accessing it a little more, it seemed. That made him smile.

"So, why are we here?" asked Dylan.

"Shh."

"Right," Dylan whispered. "Sorry."

Freddie motioned for Dylan to follow him, as he began walking between some of the foliage, toward the sun. It wasn't exactly a path, but it wasn't so dense they had to brush the greenery out of their way.

They went a couple of hundred feet, Freddie in front of Dylan, then Freddie crouched and made a gesture Dylan took to mean do the same. He got on one knee bent over a bit, which put his head below the ground shrub foliage line. After a few seconds, Dylan heard some rustling. It came closer. He also heard some faint, low grunts. It was indistinguishable. If the Stream was translating, it was just too far away to make out.

About forty feet ahead of them, Dylan saw three

Tanbacks go by, right to left. Their movement was smooth, but not quick, more systematic and deliberate, as if searching for something. Food, most likely. The Tanbacks continued on their way without pause or notice of Dylan or Freddie, and the grunting and rustling faded away.

Freddie turned and said softly, "We need to hurry a bit now." He got back up and scurried along. Dylan followed at a brisk pace. In another hundred feet, the vegetation cleared and there was a huge rock in front of them. It was twenty feet across and stuck out of the ground fifteen feet high. As they had been traveling toward the sun, they came up into the rock's shadow.

"It's almost time," said Freddie. He moved quickly around the perimeter of the rock, Dylan right behind. When they got to the far side, Freddie turned and faced the rock. "OK," he said. "In just a minute or so, this rock is going to tell us where the Arbar is."

They stood silently for a moment.

"Um, Freddie?" asked Dylan.

"Yes?"

"How is the rock going to tell us where the Arbar is?"

"When the sun is at the proper angle," said Freddie, "the current location of the Arbar is shown on this face of the rock."

"What, at this time every day?" said Dylan.

"Well, at some time of every day," Freddie answered. "The time of day when the sun is at the proper angle changes, but the sun is at the right angle at least once a day."

"How many people know about this?" Dylan said.

"Not many," said Freddie.

"So, there's a timelessly old, mystical artifact out there somewhere, probably beyond value," said Dylan, "and this rock will tell anyone who shows up where it is?"

Freddie paused. "You're right. I'm missing something. Be right back."

He vanished. He reappeared.

"Yeah," Freddie said, "we need the Holitaph. Only the Holitaph and the right sun angle will reveal where the Arbar is. But the Holitaph's with your stuff on the Zafago, isn't it?"

"Um, no," said Dylan.

"What do you mean, 'no?' Where is it?"

"On Earth," Dylan said.

"What?" yelled Freddie.

"Calm down, you'll get us eaten."

Freddie looked around. "Oh." Dylan also glanced away from the rock, and saw an impressive group of Tanbacks, maybe two hundred total, standing in a semicircle around them.

# CHAPTER 8

Dylan took a big breath of the heavy air, looked around at the grass, the Tanbacks, and the short trees and shrubs behind them, and thought about how this situation arrived.

Although Freddie's loud remark may have snapped Dylan out of the moment and into realizing the impending danger, it was obvious that wasn't what drew the Tanbacks there. There wasn't enough time for that many of them to react that fast. Something—or someone—tipped them off. Or maybe the Tanbacks knew the rock's secret, and came there every day at the right sun moment, just in case a meal showed up. Today, it did.

The Tanbacks began some grunting. It was either that or their gurgling stomachs. Either way, they began to advance on Dylan and Freddie. There was no time to wait for the sun on the rock, and they didn't have the Holitaph, anyway, so it was their moment to flash away.

"Time to get us out of here, Freddie," said Dylan.

At the moment his sentence was ending, a bright bolt of energy shot out of the sky and struck the rock. There was a huge explosion, and everything was blasted away. Dylan and Freddie and Tanbacks were all blown into the surrounding vegetation, and the rock was splintered apart into thousands of fragments, many of them no bigger than river stones, but some still quite large.

Dylan was stunned, but the thick foliage had prevented any real injury. As soon as he had his wits again, he was scanning the area for Freddie and any Tanbacks that were bent on dinner in spite of the event. He saw no Tanbacks; they seemed sufficiently shocked by the explosion to have no desire to stay. He finally located Freddie, who was frantically looking at various pieces of the rock that were lying around.

"Freddie," said Dylan, only as loud as he thought was necessary for Freddie to hear. No need to announce to any lingering Tanbacks that their meal was still alive.

"Dylan, there you are," said Freddie. "Are you OK?"

"Yeah, pretty much," said Dylan. "What're you doing?"

"Looking for a piece of the rock we can still use," Freddie said. "Over here."

Dylan rushed to him. "What is it?"

"We may still be able to use this," said Freddie. He was gesturing to a chunk of the rock that was roughly five feet across and two feet thick. "I don't know. But it's one of the bigger pieces, and one side of it is the exterior surface. It's our best chance."

"What do we do with it?" asked Dylan.

"Ready?"

Dylan blinked, and opened his eyes to see the cemetery next to Trocconics, the company where he worked. Freddie was there, and so was the chunk of rock. They were a significant distance from the road, so nobody was around. Through some trees, Dylan could see into the company parking lot enough to tell that the pile of dirt and broken asphalt created by Thergon were still there.

Although he also had enough of a vantage point to see the other direction to the intersection where the car exploded, there were no emergency vehicle lights flashing. It was late afternoon, and there'd been enough time to clear the vehicle and get the investigation moved along to where traffic was normal again. He could not see another block down the street to the collapsed warehouse. That was where the bustle of activity was, as machines busily cleared the rubble away.

"All righty, then," said Freddie. "You said the Holitaph was here?"

"Um, yeah," said Dylan, slightly startled back to the matter at hand.

"Why would you do that? What were you thinking?" asked Freddie.

"I was thinking it burned my hand," Dylan answered, "so I dropped it. You're acting like I had any idea what the hell it was."

"True," said Freddie. "So, you dropped it pretty much as soon as Thergon gave it to you?"

"Yup."

"So it's over there," said Freddie, pointing a flipper toward the parking lot.

"Yup."

"Well, there's no time to lose," Freddie said. "Shall we?"

They walked briskly across the cemetery lawn and between some trees to a fence between that and the sidewalk surrounding the edge of the parking lot.

"Well?" said Dylan.

Freddie reached his flipper out and sliced cleanly through the chain link.

"Thank you," Dylan said.

From where they were, they could see there were some temporary posts set up around Thergon's dirt pile with caution tape stretched between them.

"You need to stay here," said Dylan, "and don't let anyone see you. Go back between those trees if you need to."

"I can't protect you very easily from over here," Freddie said.

"It's a risk I'll take," Dylan replied. "There are fewer people in the plant this time of day, but if anyone sees you, or worse, sees me with you, we won't get anything accomplished before the fireballs start up again."

"All right," Freddie said. "Well, get going."

Dylan jogged across the parking lot to the dirt pile, lifted the tape, and went straight to where he was when Thergon erupted through the asphalt. The Holitaph was nowhere around. He had to look carefully, being a pitch black cube on a pile of asphalt, but it nevertheless became clear to Dylan that somebody moved it. He needed to get the word back to Freddie, but couldn't yell without a fuss, and didn't have time to go back.

He got an idea to try to use the Stream of Consciousness. He had no concept of how to do this, but he concentrated as best he could on Freddie and talking to Freddie, and quietly said, "It's not here, Freddie."

Immediately, Dylan heard Freddie say, "Wow! Nicely done. So, what, somebody took it?"

Dylan was blown away. He could communicate with Freddie through the Stream! "Yeah," he said. "Could be the police, but I got an idea." He started toward the building.

"No," Freddie said. "No time for that."

"Hang on," said Dylan, already approaching the plant doors.

He went inside, and made his way through the maze of cubicles toward his desk. As he passed each one, he glanced inside to see if there was any clue of anything or anyone that could help. Most were empty and normal looking, a few had people typing or clicking away, without notice.

He got to his cubicle group, and saw that Matt Claremore, at the desk next to his, was still working.

"Hey, Matt," said Dylan.

"Wow, what happened to you?" Matt said. "You went down to get your phone and nobody saw you again. Then that thing in the parking lot."

"Yeah, that's weird, eh?" Dylan said.

"I'll say. It was like a sink hole, only opposite. Don't know what they call those."

"Were you guys out there?" asked Dylan.

"Yeah, after it happened," said Matt. "Pretty wild. Big traffic jam, people all over. You didn't see it?"

"Nah, I had to leave. Family message on my phone," said Dylan. "Say, this might seem like a weird question, but did anybody happen to see a black stone cube out there on the ground?"

"Yeah, as a matter of fact," said Matt. "How did you know? Barbara found it."

Dylan started to move away to Barbara's desk. "She's not there," Matt called after. "She started feeling sick and went home."

"OK," Dylan called back. "Thanks, Matt."

Dylan quickly stepped over to Barbara's cubicle. It was on her desk! He snatched it up and looked around. Nobody could see him. He had to be running desperately low on time before his enemies knew he was there. Holding the Holitaph was already making him feel energized, and now was the time to try to use the Stream of Consciousness to teleport himself.

He stood up straight, closed his eyes, and concentrated on being on the cemetery property where Freddie was. He opened them just in time to watch from the cemetery as a lightning ball landed on the electronics plant. Nearly half the building was immediately demolished in an enormous explosion. A huge fireball erupted, and the walls were splintered like matchsticks.

Dylan's knees buckled, and the shock wave from the explosion knocked him over, even that far away. He lay there, stunned.

"Dylan," said Freddie, "This is horrible. I know this is horrible. I can't believe I have to say this, but there is no time to react to what you just saw. We have to move."

"Freddie..." Dylan said. The deadly seriousness of the

mission he was on just hit home in a staggering way. Dancing around the danger on his own behalf, or with Freddie, just wasn't completely real yet. He was still in that movie. But watching his workplace disintegrate, knowing dozens of people he worked with every day were just instantly killed, was a devastating blow.

"I know," said Freddie. "Please believe I feel your shock and pain, but we have to move. Don't let those people die in vain."

"My God," said Dylan, "my God."

"Come on," said Freddie, lifting Dylan's shoulders.

"All right," Dylan said as he began to sit up on his own. He turned onto one knee and got to his feet as the two of them began running to the rock. Freddie raised a flipper as a lightning ball hit it and flared in a plume of brilliant flame. "Can't you do it from here?" Dylan yelled.

"It's harder," said Freddie, chugging along. "Can't you?"

"Very funny," said Dylan. Another energy ball came down, another deflection by Freddie.

They reached the rock. "OK," Freddie said, exhaling heavily.

Dylan was looking out of the mouth of a large cave, at a pink sky framed by a few gnarled branches of some trees with long needles. They made Dylan think of a pine tree on steroids. Catching his breath, he dropped from his stance and sat on the chunk of rock they brought with them. This constant barrage of sensory input was overloading him, on top of watching his work building demolished.

"So, where's this?" Dylan said, almost as if he was only asking because he was expected to. He was obviously spent.

"Just get your breath, Dylan," said Freddie, panting. "We're OK here for a bit."

"Freddie," said Dylan.

"Yeah?"

Dylan paused. "I don't know. I don't know."

"Everything's going to be all right," Freddie said. "Just

let the Holitaph help you get your head straight."

Dylan didn't answer. He wanted to be done with all this. He wanted to be at home, with his chair at home, watching football with a beer and a chicken pot pie.

He still had the holitaph in his right hand, and he looked down at it, first with a mind to blaming it for everything, then more intently concentrating on it and considering what it could be.

Freddie was right about the Holitaph. It was the weirdest thing. It wasn't like a drug or anything, but it really was an energizing, invigorating, focusing influence. Besides the physical energy, it seemed to clear away emotional confusion. Not reduce emotional impact, just make the perspective clear. Help him understand that yes, the death of his workmates is intolerably needless and evil. And yes, it is appropriate to mourn the loss and reflect on that evil.

But no, moving forward with urgent tasks does not minimize the acknowledgement of the event. On the contrary, it shows the greater capacity to act with a clear head in the face of something that could help the evil win by dwelling on the emotional. The Holitaph helped Dylan understand that the most honorable reaction to the deaths of his colleagues was focused action against the perpetrators. Not emotional, irrational, vengeful action, but focused, effective, calculated action.

"All right," Dylan said. "What do we do with the rock?"

There was no answer.

"Freddie?"

He looked around. Freddie was gone. He was probably off hob-knobbing with his fellow Panel members while Dylan collected his thoughts. Dylan was a little surprised that Freddie hadn't said something, but no matter. He'd be back in a matter of moments, more than likely.

Dylan then remembered the Stream. If he could talk to Freddie across a parking lot, he could do it across the galaxy, or across the universe. He focused his concentration on talking to Freddie, and said, "Where are you, Freddie?"

There was still no answer. Oh, well. Dylan knew Freddie kept himself out of the Stream intentionally when it suited him, so he was probably offline, so to speak. No big deal. He sat on the rock, waiting for Freddie to show up.

After a few moments, he heard a startling voice in his head. It was deep and slow.

"Dylan, I am Merdal. I am the rightful owner of the Holitaph you hold. It was stolen from me by Thergon, and I ask for its return."

This was another first: a different voice, someone he'd obviously never met, contacting him through the Stream of Consciousness. The initial surprise had already subsided by the time the voice was finished, and Dylan was alertly processing the information.

"No," said Dylan. "You stole it from Xarnicus. You are not the rightful owner." This was a bit of a guess on his part, as far as the identity of the thief of Xarnicus, but he threw it out there.

"I recovered it," said Merdal. "I am the creator of the Holitaph. Xarnicus held it for eons, but it was not his. It is mine."

Dylan's mental focus was sharp. He recognized that if the Holitaph was everything Freddie was saying it was, and the being speaking to him really did create it, that being would be incredibly and multi-dimensionally powerful. He also recognized that he would not be able to accomplish anything in this conversation if he felt or acted intimidated by that power.

"Wrong again," Dylan said. His boldness was fueled both by the improvisational movie concept he was recovering in his attitude, and the feeling of empowered detachment from conversing through the Stream instead of face-to-face.

"The creator of the Holitaph was killed," Dylan continued. "It's not you."

"I was thought dead," Merdal continued, "but instead

was relegated to the fourteenth dimension until I could determine a method to enter the other dimensions again. I have done so, and I am here to reclaim my property."

Dylan got even bolder, perhaps more than he was prepared to deal with. "Come and get it, then," he said. He had no idea what he would do if Merdal complied, especially without Freddie there.

"As you wish," said Merdal.

Oops.

# CHAPTER 9

At the mouth of it, the cave was about the size of a two-car garage, only taller, like an RV would fit. The rock that formed it had stunning striations of light orange and deep red. The back of the cave tapered downhill into darkness. Dylan was seated a car-length from the mouth, a bit to one side, on the rock he and Freddie brought from Balytre, where the Tanbacks were.

Merdal instantly appeared in the cave, just a few feet from Dylan. He looked exactly like Thergon—body with three tentacles, football head, everything.

"You will return the Holitaph now," he said.

"Ah," said Dylan, standing up and trying to sound less unnerved than he felt at having his bluff called. "I've met your kind before."

"Thergon was much younger and less…talented than I," said Merdal, "but yes, we are the same species."

"So," Dylan said, holding up the Holitaph, "this is yours?"

"Yes," said Merdal. "Return it now."

"Your type doesn't strike me as a dawdler," Dylan said.

"Why haven't you taken it?"

"The Stream," Merdal answered. "Do not trifle with me, human. You have developed some crude abilities with the Stream. If I attempt to use physical means, you ride the Stream. I refuse to engage in such games."

"If I'm in the Stream," asked Dylan, "why not just grab me and put me wherever you are, then kill me?"

"The Holitaph has many wondrous properties," said Merdal. "Among them are some protections from vulnerabilities associated with being in the Stream. With some effort, I can still locate you, but I cannot transport you while you are bonded with the Holitaph. It is also protecting you from some types of projectile injury. Otherwise, you would already be dead. The energy bursts directed at you were not off target."

*Wow, this guy is oversharing. He doesn't seem like the stupid type, so he must be the classically overconfident evil type. He's too proud of the Holitaph he made not to brag about it. Freddie was wrong. Some of this is happening exactly like in the movies.*

"What do you mean, you can't transport me?" said Dylan. "Freddie's been doing it whenever he pleases."

"As the creator of the Holitaph, my relationship with it is unique, including elements that transcend the fourteenth dimension. Some aspects of this are empowering, some are limiting."

"Fine," said Dylan, "so the Holitaph is protecting me. If you're the one who's been shooting those flame balls at me, but you knew they couldn't actually hit me, what's the point?"

"A direct hit is not the only method of ending your life," said Merdal. "Would you not have died from the crumbling warehouse? Or in the building where so many of your worthless workmates were eradicated?"

This riled Dylan quite a bit. Merdal not only didn't care that he was killing people on a whim, he considered them pests.

"So, it looks we've already moved past the whole rational

motivation thing, you ridiculous oaf," said Dylan. Yes, Merdal had pretty much given away his hand by not attempting first to get Dylan to hand over the Holitaph through a sense of honor and fair play, returning it to its rightful owner. Even if Merdal did create the Holitaph, Dylan certainly suspected he was after it for no good.

Merdal sounded a bit more irritated. "The Holitaph is mine. Return it."

"Let's say you're right, and it's yours," said Dylan. "There's talk this thing accesses the fourteenth dimension, and would allow for all sorts of crazy stuff like altering time in small parts of the universe. True?"

"You are correct," said Merdal. "The Holitaph's properties engaging the fourteenth dimension are unique in the universe. It is a singular and powerful artifact." He patted a tentacle on the side of the rock Dylan had been sitting on. "It's relationship to this rock, for instance. The Holitaph has no equivalent."

"Answer me this," Dylan said. "Would you give a serial killer his gun just because it was his?"

"Enough," said Merdal. "You will comply, or Freddie dies."

"Freddie? You know where Freddie is?"

"Freddie is on my ship. You cannot reach him through the Stream, nor he you. I have captured him, and your dallinite escape pod is now his prison cell. Give me the Holitaph now or he dies."

*So Freddie didn't go anywhere on his own. He was kidnapped. No wonder Merdal hasn't been trying to finesse the Holitaph from me, with this card to play. How could he even do that? Freddie's right, this guy has some dark powers. This is a twisted situation, but Merdal has to be at least partially bluffing. If he kills Freddie, his bargaining chip is gone.*

"No," Dylan said. "I have to go now."

"Consider it, and you will realize you have no choice," said Merdal. "Find my consciousness in the Stream, and you can come to my ship to return my Holitaph. Do it or Freddie dies."

"Yeah, you said that."

Merdal disappeared. Dylan was planning to try to use the Stream for a getaway, but evidently Merdal had more of a need for the dramatic exit.

The situation with Freddie notwithstanding, this probably meant at least one good thing. It felt more unlikely Dylan would get bombarded with attacks everywhere he went. Merdal was apparently wanting him to be in his ship, where he would not be using "projectile injury" to kill Dylan. Some other plan, no doubt.

As long as Merdal's goal was to kill Dylan, it also seemed likely there would be some other type of warning before Freddie would actually be harmed, assuming Merdal could even pull that off. Freddie wasn't exactly easy to kill. A bargaining chip is useless unless it is played, and Merdal would certainly have more taunting and threatening to do before he acted. Not discounting Freddie's danger, there was at least some amount of time and notice to be had before the situation to save Freddie was truly critical.

Uncertain what to do next, Dylan walked slowly over the last few feet to the mouth of the cave, to see more of where he was.

The vista was extraordinary. The general terrain was dry and rocky, and the cave appeared to be somewhere around half-way up a substantial mountain. Straight ahead was a small, flat area just outside the cave, then the sloping mountainside down to a valley. That hill, and off to his right, hosted a generous scattering of medium-tall trees with very thick trunks and gnarled branches sporting long, thick needles.

To his left was the most impressive: a series of staggeringly beautiful, dark red mountains from which sprang tall, spiraling rock formations in brilliant red and orange. Between two of the mountains was a wide, breathtaking waterfall, landing in a riverbed that flowed through the lower foothills into the valley and joined another river flowing the length of the valley and off into the distance.

This was instantly one of Dylan's favorite places in the universe.

He imagined a day without everything else, when he could use the Stream to pop here on a Saturday afternoon with a grill, hot dogs, a cooler, and a lounge chair. Were he lacking the Holitaph to help focus his thoughts, he would only have needed to step out here to put everything at peace.

Dylan heard a noise from the sky. It was vaguely familiar. He stepped out a little farther so he could turn around and see more of the rest of the mountain above him. Rising over it was the Zafago.

*Ha! Urbor found me! This is going to be a huge help.*

The ship continued descending to the hillside a little ways below him, positioning to miss trees. Dylan could see that the landing gear extended farther on the lower side, so the ship would land level. It settled there, and the hatch opened. Urbor and two other lenthers stepped down the plank.

Dylan moved down the hillside. "Urbor!"

"Dylan, my friend," said Urbor. "Come aboard."

"Not just yet," said Dylan as they met near the bottom of the ramp. He explained about the rock from the Tanbacks' planet, Balytre, and the attack and explosion and everything. The rock needed to come with them.

"Where is Freddie?" Urbor asked during the conversation.

"He won't be here," said Dylan. "That's our next order of business. I'll explain over some millis."

Urbor arranged for several crew members to go up to the cave with some equipment and a cargo pallet that could accommodate the rock. They loaded it up and hauled it onto the Zafago.

Once they were underway, Urbor and Freddie retired to the diplomatic room to discuss next moves.

"So," Freddie started. "How did you find me? And why?"

"For a time after you jettisoned," said Urbor, "we remained in stealth mode, of course. Then, it became time to venture into the Stream and see if you had landed safely."

"How could you do that from the Zafago?" said Dylan.

"Generally, protection from intrusive use of the Stream is good, but access becomes a necessity from time to time, of course. There is an exposure bubble, a protrusion on the side of the ship that specifically allows one to be outside the dallinite and use the Stream. It is unavailable in stealth mode, but once we opened the windows again I could make use of it.

"At that time, you were on Earth. That was not where we expected, but it meant you were safe. It seems you had already been through your entire adventure on Balytre."

Dylan was subdued. "Yes," he said.

"Is there something troubling you about that?" asked Urbor.

"Well, things happen so fast," Dylan said, "that taking time for stuff to soak in just isn't possible, but there was a catastrophe on Earth, and you mentioning that you sensed us there reminded me."

"What happened on Earth?"

Dylan explained the recovery of the Holitaph, and the narrow escape while his company's building was destroyed with many people inside.

"Dylan, I am truly sorry for your loss," said Urbor. He raised his glass of millis.

Dylan raised his and said, "We share in the honor of the lives of my colleagues that were taken before their time."

"In their honor we share," said Urbor. They drank.

"It is quite good news that you were able to recover the Holitaph," Urbor continued, "and, I might add, that you have successfully expanded your use of the Stream to include transporting yourself. That may prove critical in the time ahead of us."

"In a way, it already has," said Dylan.

"In what way?"

"Well, that brings me to Freddie," said Dylan. He proceeded into the story of Merdal kidnapping Freddie, and how Merdal had not attempted to simply take the Holitaph by force because of Dylan's use of the Stream.

"Well, well," said Urbor. "You are quite an impressive man. So, this Merdal identified himself as the legendary creator of the Holitaph, come back from the fourteenth dimension. Mark me, if Merdal is who he claims to be, your experience is a harbinger of deep foreboding for the universe. You deftly escaped your encounter with an incredibly skilled sorcerer. Many would not."

"I'm sure it was just the Holitaph," Dylan said.

"Perhaps," Urbor said, "but I am impressed nevertheless."

Dylan was incredibly pleased to be in Urbor's good graces, but gloating was sure to be one way to change that in a hurry. He shifted the subject. "So, what do we do about Freddie?" he said.

"Locating him will not be a problem," said Urbor. "Merdal undoubtedly has the capability of blocking himself from the Stream, but he has made it clear he expects you to find him, so I doubt he is doing so." He paused in thought. "No, the problem is not locating Freddie. The problem is that they are likely very far away, farther than the Zafago can travel in the time we need. Merdal would not have invited you to his ship if he thought any substantial assistance could accompany you."

"Can we move the ship through the Stream?" asked Dylan.

"Regrettably, no," answered Urbor. "The size is a concern, but one that could be dealt with. The real problem is the dallinite. Merdal seems to have solved that difficulty, but we have not."

"What should we do, then?" Dylan said.

The doors opened and one of the crew stepped in. "Leader," he said, "some of the crew is very sick. It happened quite quickly. You should review their condition with the medical staff."

"This does not sound good," Urbor said to Dylan. "Come."

Urbor got up and moved out of the room, Dylan following. With the other lenther who made the announcement, they went down the corridor and down two ramps, then down a gently curving corridor past several sets of doors with various markings on them, until they reached a pair of doors on the right. Urbor opened them and stepped in. This was the infirmary.

The entry room had windows directly ahead, looking into an examination area, with a short, curved hall to the left and right around the windows. Doors at the end of each hall allowed entry to the exam area. Dylan saw several lenthers lying on pads on the floor, and several others tending them in various ways, with equipment hanging on posts that could be wheeled around the room. Display screens with odd pictures, wave forms, and other sorts of information were on the wall behind them.

Urbor continued through the doors to the left of the window, but motioned for Dylan to remain in the observation room. The other lenther went to the right and through the doors there, then joined the caregivers in conversation with Urbor once they were gathered in the exam area.

Dylan could only hear muffled sounds, but Urbor looked disappointed and upset as the conversation moved along. It went on for several minutes, then Urbor walked among the afflicted patients, speaking to them briefly. When he had addressed each of them, he came back out to the observation room.

"This is quite upsetting," he said to Dylan. "They are severely ill."

"What is it?" asked Dylan.

"We don't know yet," said Urbor. "The symptoms are not unusual, but the speed and severity of the onset is. Our staff is analyzing blood samples. They'll have an answer soon."

The doors from the corridor into the observation room burst open, and another lenther staggered in, obviously ill. He took a couple of steps and collapsed to the floor.

"Barhod!" Urbor exclaimed. He waved into the exam area, and two of the medical staff came rushing out to assist the newest patient. They managed to get him to his feet and help him into the exam room.

"That was my first commander, Barhod," said Urbor. "This is very serious."

One of the staff in the exam room caught Urbor's attention with a frantic gesture. Urbor turned and hurried in. Several lenthers were showing Urbor something on the wall screens, urgently pointing and speaking emphatically. Urbor was also waving his arms and shouting for a moment, then he became calm again. He appeared to relay some stern commands, then came back out to the observation room.

"Dylan," he said. "Dylan, this is dire. We are in very grave danger."

"What? What is it?" said Dylan.

Two of the medical staff hurried past Dylan and Urbor and out into the corridor.

"Dylan," Urbor began again, "where did you say that rock came from?"

"Balytre," answered Dylan. "Why?"

"This is most disturbing," said Urbor. "These men are afflicted with daubitira. Have you heard of it?"

"I'm sorry, no," said Dylan.

"It does not exist on Earth," Urbor explained. "But it also does not exist on Balytre. In fact, daubitira comes from a section of the universe altogether removed from anywhere you have been."

"I'm presuming from your tone," Dylan said, "that daubitira is a serious illness."

"You presume correctly. It is one of the deadliest diseases in the medical archives."

A voice came over the speaker in the control panel next to

the corridor doors.

"Alert, Leader."

Urbor went to it and pushed a button.

"Acknowledge."

"Please come to cargo hold Gart One," said the voice.

"I shall," said Urbor. "Join me," he said to Dylan as he stepped out into the corridor.

They moved briskly up two ramps and a long way down a straight corridor. "Gart One is where your rock is being stored," said Urbor. "Something seems to be amiss."

They arrived at the cargo hold, and the two medical staff members who had rushed out of the exam room were standing with the rock and holding some devices. "Observe, Leader," one of them said.

"What is it?" said Urbor.

"Here, on the rock," the other lenther said, gesturing at the side of it. "It is very small, but there is a deposit of wet material there," he continued. "It is contaminated with daubitira."

They were all silent for a moment, pondering what this could mean and how it could have gotten there.

"Dylan," said Urbor, "describe the movements of the rock one more time, please."

"Sure," said Dylan. "First, Freddie and I were on Balytre with the entire rock, and the energy bolt blew it apart. We took this chunk of it to Earth, and it sat in the cemetery while we retrieved the Holitaph. Then we took it to the planet where you picked me up. I don't know the name of that one."

"It is called Verwen," said Urbor. "But to the rock. Was anyone else ever with you?"

Dylan paused in thought. "Merdal!"

"He is the only one?" asked Urbor.

"Yes," said Dylan, "and he touched it. It was so him! He reached out and patted the rock with his tentacle while we were talking. No wonder he was so quick to leave. He was trying not to catch the daubitira he was planting on the rock!"

"I agree," said Urbor. "I would say he must have had a container that would dissolve shortly after exposure to atmosphere. If he was planting it intentionally, he would never have risked actually touching the contaminated substance."

"So what does this mean?" said Dylan.

"It means—"

Urbor stopped because both of the medics collapsed to the floor.

# CHAPTER 10

Urbor rushed out of the cargo hold. "We must hurry," he said.

"Are they dead?" asked Dylan, hastening behind Urbor.

As they moved back down the corridor, Urbor continued explaining. "Not yet, but they don't have long. Daubitira is one of the most virulent and rapidly infectious diseases in the universe. It kills with alarming speed. We only have one option."

"Shouldn't we be quarantining ourselves?" said Dylan.

"There is no point," Urbor said. "As soon as my staff informed me this was daubitira, there was nothing to be gained by attempting to contain it. By that time, everyone on board must be considered exposed."

He stopped in the middle of the corridor. "Which brings up a curiosity. You have been exposed the longest of anyone. How do you feel?"

"Um, normal," said Dylan.

"That is exceedingly fortunate," said Urbor, turning to continue down the corridor.

"Where are we going?" Dylan asked.

"The daubitira is going to kill everyone on board, including you and me," Urbor said, "but I know someone who may be able to help. He has medical and mystical skills that equal or exceed all other doctors or scientists I have known. We must get to him."

So much had happened to Dylan, with so many unexpected turns, that he wasn't really grasping the message that he had just contracted a fatal disease. He heard it, and would act on it, but he somehow didn't really accept that he could be living his final minutes. What he was thinking about was where they were on the ship. Dylan had tried to pay enough attention to the corridors that he had a vague concept of what was where. "Isn't the bridge above us?" he said.

"We are not going to the bridge," said Urbor. "This ship is too far away from Doctor Habian to get us there in time, and it cannot be transported using the Stream of Consciousness. We will use the satellite craft."

As Urbor finished speaking, he turned through doors on the left and entered another dock room. This one was quite a bit larger than the others Dylan had seen, and it contained a small ship.

"Oh, yeah," said Dylan, "Freddie mentioned this utility ship. Cool."

The ship was about as big around as a pickup truck, but twice as long. It was sleek, with ridges protruding from the sides that suggested wings, but not as wide as those of any aircraft Dylan had seen on Earth. On top was a clear bubble providing full visibility for the pilots. There was seating for two, side by side, with controls in front of each, but the seating was only lenther pads on the floor of the compartment.

The transparent cockpit roof lifted up, and Urbor climbed in. "Quickly," he said. "I should tell you that I can feel the effects of the daubitira, and we must get off this ship at once. I apologize that there is no chair accommodations for you.

There is no time."

"Not a problem," said Dylan as he climbed in next to Urbor and sat on the second pad, with his legs crossed in front of him.

The roof closed as Urbor was pushing some control buttons. As soon as it latched, a panel in the side of the Zafago opened for them to exit. The ship lifted slightly, then glided forward.

The moment they had cleared the shell of the Zafago, the stars in front of them changed, and Dylan could see a nearby planet of blue and green off to their left. Urbor had used the Stream to transport them.

"Is that Doctor Habian's planet?" Dylan asked.

Urbor didn't answer. Dylan looked over at him, and he was slumped against the clear bubble, unconscious.

*No! What the hell do I do now?*

He pushed gently on Urbor's shoulder to roust him. "Urbor!" There was no response.

*The Stream. I can talk to Urbor through the Stream.*

Dylan tried to concentrate on Urbor. "Urbor," he said, "can you hear me?"

He didn't hear any response, and didn't feel any connection to Urbor.

*Oh, right. Duh. It's the Stream of Consciousness. If you're unconscious, you aren't in the Stream. Great.*

Dylan glanced around at the controls in front of him. Flying this thing was a ridiculous notion, but what could he lose by trying to do something? He'd be dead of daubitira in a little while, anyway—why not go down in a crash?

All of the controls were identified with lenther symbols. There were mostly buttons of various sizes and illuminated colors, with a joystick in the middle and a few rotary knobs on his right. The most instinctive thing to do was grab the joystick and see if that did anything. He grabbed it and moved it slowly to the left. No change he could see. He moved it to the right. No change. He pulled it toward himself, and pushed it away. No change. A little exasperated, he waved it quickly around in circles. No change.

Dylan heard a voice. "Hello, Dylan," it said.

"Hello?" said Dylan.

He heard it again, in a soothing, conversational tone. "I am Doctor Habian."

"Wow! Doctor Habian!" said Dylan. "Where are you?"

"I am on the planet below you," said Habian.

"Do you know Urbor?" said Dylan.

"Yes, I certainly do," Doctor Habian answered. "Why isn't he in the Stream? Is he unconscious from the disease already?"

"You know about that?" said Dylan.

"I do," said the Doctor. "He contacted me briefly to let me know of the daubitira and that you were with him. It helped a great deal in finding you in the Stream."

"Well, it's a problem," said Dylan. "Yes, Urbor is passed out."

"Oh, dear," said Habian. "We need to get you down here immediately."

"I know, I know," Dylan said, "but I can't fly this thing."

"Are you sure?" asked the Doctor. "I can bring you down through the Stream, but not Urbor, in his unconscious state."

"I'm not coming down there without him."

"Could you do it, since you can see where he is?" Habian said.

"Through the Stream? Oh, boy, I don't know. I haven't moved somebody else yet. If I did it wrong...I can't risk that."

"If I bring the whole ship down here while it's flying, you'll just crash into everything," Habian said.

"The controls are all lenther symbols," said Dylan, "and all the lenthers I've met are either unconscious or on a ship shielded in dallinite."

"Then reach out to some you haven't met," said Doctor Habian.

Dylan hadn't tried to intentionally use the Stream this

way, yet. He concentrated on letting his thoughts drift to any collective lenther presence in the Stream. After a moment, he became aware of their home world. And all the ship's controls turned to English.

"Awesome!" Dylan said. "It worked. I see one lit up that says 'Auto.'" He pushed it, and the illumination turned off. He grabbed the joystick again and began moving it gently. The ship responded in kind, rolling smoothly to the left, then the right, as the joystick went. "Haha! I can steer the ship now!"

"Wonderful," said Doctor Habian. "If you can bring it closer to the planet's surface, I can guide you. When you get close enough to our facility, our landing dock's guidance system can connect to your automatic controls for the last few hundred feet and land you safely."

"Outstanding," said Dylan.

Doctor Habian talked Dylan through his descent. Dylan figured out a few other controls, adjusting the speed as necessary to enter the atmosphere without complications, all with the Doctor's instructions. It took some time, and Dylan was concerned about Urbor and the rest of the lenthers on the Zafago, but eventually he came within guidance distance of Doctor Habian's lab, and the facility's system brought the utility ship into the dock.

The landing dock was like a large carport, attached to a large, circular building of brushed steel and windows, with doors to the landing area. Dylan found the button to pop the cockpit roof. As it lifted, Dylan could see several beings running out from the building doors toward the ship. They looked remarkably human.

*Humanoids! About flippin' time!*

"Stop!" Dylan yelled. "Daubitira!"

"It's OK," one of the running men called back.

As they got nearer, Dylan could see that their skin color was a creamy pink, and their eyes were slightly larger than human eyes, but this species was clearly much closer to human than any he'd met yet.

"Quickly! Quickly!" said one of them as they reached the ship. Dylan recognized Doctor Habian's voice.

"Get Urbor!" said Dylan, climbing out of the ship. He was on the far side of it from the building, and he ran around to help lift Urbor out and carry him.

"Into the main lab," said Doctor Habian as they went back through the doors carrying Urbor. The main lab was dead ahead down a long, wide hallway. Near the doors was a platform with several chairs and a padded table surface, situated on the end of a conveyor. They placed Urbor gently on the table and quickly sat as the platform began moving swiftly down the conveyor.

They passed what appeared to be an elevator, an administrator at a desk, then numerous rooms and hallways to other parts of the facility branching off in a curve on either side. The conveyor slowed to a rest just outside a set of double doors swinging into what seemed to be the main lab, at the core of the circular facility. They lifted Urbor once again and barreled through the doors.

"The lower exam table," Habian instructed as they brought Urbor a short distance to a knee-high, padded table large enough to lay him on.

"Vitals," said the Doctor to the others who had been helping. They hustled around collecting equipment and attaching things to Urbor, including a mask that provided a higher concentration of oxygen.

Doctor Habian and the others varied in height from perhaps five-feet-eight to six feet, and slender but not anorexic. Up close, Dylan got a better look at their skin, a smooth, pearly pink. Their eyes were indeed slightly larger than human eyes, and their ears slightly smaller, but hair, teeth, noses, and everything else about their movement and manner could be mistaken for human. They were dressed in green, full-length, spandex pants and blue form-fitting coats all alike, which Dylan hoped was some kind of work uniform or lab smock, and not indicative of social fashion.

"Now, about you, young man," Doctor Habian said to Dylan. "Please sit."

There were several stools of acceptable height in a row along the wall behind Urbor, and Dylan accommodated.

The room was large, perhaps sixty feet across, forming a semicircle around one more small room in the center. It was scattered with an intriguing array of examination furniture and robotic-looking equipment. The medical lab on the Zafago was brightly lit, but this one was done more in task lighting, with spotlights on tables, stools, and the like, but the room essentially dim otherwise. The coloration of the walls was pink, and Dylan thought it was interesting that a color like beige was so popular for European humans and more pink here with these people, perhaps matching an inherent psychological connection with skin tone. Assuming the intention was to help keep people relaxed, it wasn't working with Dylan.

"Why aren't we in quarantine?" said Dylan. "Urbor said this thing was incredibly infectious."

"Infectious, yes," said Doctor Habian, "communicable, no. Daubitira is so deadly because it does travel by air and because a single infected cell usually kills. But it does not manifest in the cardiopulmonary system, and thus is not given to transfer through exhaling, coughing, sneezing, and the like. Nor by touch."

"What does it do?" Dylan asked.

"It instantly finds and latches onto navanizone," said the Doctor.

"What's that?" said Dylan.

Habian got a quizzical look on his face. "Navanizone is the primary hormone regulating and maximizing oxygen transfer between cells." Dylan still had a blank look on his face. "It's made by your polydyx."

"My what?" said Dylan.

"Your polydyx." Habian paused. "You do have a

polydyx, don't you?"

"Never heard of it," said Dylan, "but I'm no anatomy expert."

Doctor Habian called to one of the other men. "Furmascope!" The assistant flung open a drawer and brought a device that looked like one of the electronic voltage meters Dylan used at work. Habian flipped it open.

"Sit up straight," he said to Dylan. He held the device forward and scanned Dylan's chest and abdomen.

"Holy Wackinoly," he said. He looked at the assistant. "Kerlan, this man has no polydyx." He turned back to Dylan. "How do you process oxygen? I've never seen an oxygen-breathing species without a polydyx. This is remarkable."

"I don't know, Doc," said Dylan. "I breathe, my lungs fill up, and the blood flows through there and gets oxygen. After that, I don't know."

"Well, well, well," said the Doctor. "I'm not one to argue with good fortune. We need your blood immediately. May we?"

"Um, sure, but why?" said Dylan. "What good fortune?"

Kerlan began collecting equipment to take some blood from Dylan.

"If you have no polydyx," said Doctor Habian, "you have no navanizone. The mystery of your survival notwithstanding, if you have no navanizone, you are immune to daubitira. And that means your body is free to produce antibodies to destroy the daubitira, without all the annoying biological distractions like death. In short, sir, you are a miracle."

"Boy am I glad to hear that," said Dylan.

"Me, too," agreed Habian.

"Me, too, Daddy," said an approaching voice.

"Ah, my dear," said the Doctor, looking behind him. "Yes, this will fascinate you." He turned to Dylan. "Dylan, meet the other Doctor Habian. My daughter, Faldra. Faldra, this is Dylan, our newest medical marvel."

Faldra stepped up to Doctor Habian's side. She was spectacularly beautiful. Her skin seemed to almost glow, and the larger eyes were a magnificent feature, framed by soft, waving, shoulder-length black hair. Her eyes were a light orange-brown color Dylan had never seen the likes of in a human. Dylan also noticed that the form-fitting lab attire on her tall figure suddenly became a far more acceptable fashion in his view.

"A pleasure to meet you," said Faldra, extending a hand.

Dylan grasped her hand, but chose not to shake or move it, not knowing what sort of customs these people had. He risked it with Urbor, but was instantly more careful, and more nervous about it, around Faldra. In the middle of everything that had happened, the last thing he expected to encounter was a captivating woman.

"The pleasure is mine," he said. Kerlan was now wrapping a cuff around his arm, with a tube extending to a vial. As soon as it was attached, blood started flowing down the tube, but Dylan felt nothing beyond the cuff itself.

"I came as soon as I saw your scan in our system," Faldra said. "Not to make you feel like a specimen, but there's a lot we can learn from you."

Dylan smiled and ran a hand through his hair. "And believe me, I would love to contribute to your knowledge base," said Dylan, "but I'm in an urgent situation. I can't spend a lot of time here."

Kerlan disconnected the cuff, capped the vial, and rushed off through a door in the back of the lab. As he left, Faldra called over her shoulder, "Thank you, Kerlan." Kerlan waved a hand in acknowledgement on his way out.

"I'm aware of the situation with Freddie, and the Holitaph, and Merdal, and the Galderinx," said Doctor Habian.

Dylan looked surprised. "Galderinx?"

"Freddie is being held on a Galderinx ship," said Habian. Dylan remembered back to his first time on Urbor's ship, and that it was the Galderinx that had approached with scouts. Merdal must have enlisted the Galderinx as minions.

"I apologize for the intrusion into your thoughts," Doctor Habian continued. " I wouldn't have, but our extended conversation while you were flying the utility craft made it impossible not to see other things going on in your mind, and therefore in the Stream."

*Note to self: using the Stream to deliberately probe someone's thoughts is considered bad form. By some, at least.*

"Quite all right," Dylan replied. "So you know I need to go get Freddie right away. You have my blood, right? You can use that to help Urbor and the other lenthers?"

"Perhaps," Faldra said, "but not necessarily. We need to talk about this."

# CHAPTER 11

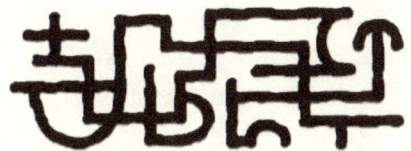

Dylan looked absently around Doctor Habian's lab as he adjusted his weight on his stool and considered what "We need to talk about this" might mean. Aside from not leaving immediately to free Freddie, that is, which seemed apparent. He wasn't too wild about that, and he could tell from Faldra's reaction that it showed, but he was willing to listen.

Faldra leaned slightly toward Dylan and spoke pleadingly. "Urbor does not have long to live, nor do the others on his ship," she explained. "We can try to make a serum from your blood, but if it doesn't work, or we can't make it in time, we need to try a direct transfusion between you and Urbor."

"I see," said Dylan.

"Freddie needs to be freed," said Doctor Habian, "but he will stay alive until you can help him. They can't risk taking him out of the dallinite pod, and Merdal knows full well they have no bait to lure you any more if he dies."

"Hm. That's true," Dylan said.

"Please," said Faldra, "Your intentions to help Freddie as quickly as possible are wonderful, and I admire that very much, but Urbor's life may still depend on you staying here a little longer until we know what we have."

Running around on adventures, reacting to whatever comes your way, was one thing. Making life-and-death decisions was another. Freddie would have to understand.

"Yes, of course," Dylan said. "We'll make sure Urbor has the best chance to pull through this."

Faldra took his hand. "Thank you."

"Now. We have lots of work to do with that serum," said Doctor Habian. "In the meantime, Dylan, if you're going off to rescue Freddie, no offense, but you could use some practice navigating the Stream of Consciousness."

"It's that obvious?" said Dylan.

Faldra chuckled a little.

"Point taken," Dylan continued. "How do I do that?"

"Faldra, my dear," said Habian, "take Dylan to the large activity room and help him become more familiar with using the Stream, would you?"

"With pleasure," she said. "Come on, Dylan."

Dylan got up from the stool and followed Faldra out of the lab and down one of the hallways branching off the main area. They reached a room on the right, and went in. There were tables and chairs, a few floor-standing machines that looked like exercise equipment, and a countertop along one wall that had a sink and some cupboards.

"OK," said Faldra. "So is it true you are in the Stream because you have the Holitaph?"

"Yup," Dylan said. "Ever heard about it before?"

"Only in childhood stories," Faldra said. "It's really amazing to me if it truly exists. Can I see it?"

"Um, I don't have it on me," said Dylan. "It's on Urbor's ship right now."

"Goodness," Faldra replied, "aren't you worried about someone else taking it?"

Dylan inhaled deeply, expanding his chest. "Nah," he said, "if anyone holds it too long, it kills 'em. They're not bonded to it the way I am."

"I see," said Faldra with a smile. "But you're in the Stream all the time, anyway?"

"Yes," Dylan said. "Doesn't matter where the Holitaph is."

"All right, then," she said, "Let's see. What have you done so far?"

"Oh, well…" Dylan mused, "I moved a chair, and myself once, about a thousand feet. And I've had conversations with people, like your father."

"That's it?"

"Well, sure," said Dylan.

"OK, we'll start with something small," said Faldra. "See that cup over on the counter? Move that into your hand."

"Right." Dylan stared at the cup, and in just a moment, it appeared in his right hand.

"Very nice," Faldra said. "Looks like we need to work on speed, and non-focused stuff."

"Non-focused?"

"Not having to look at the cup to move it."

"Oh. Right."

Over the next fifteen minutes, Faldra ran Dylan through a series of exercises, moving himself, the cup, himself and the cup simultaneously, then doing things faster and faster, until he was popping around the room with or without the cup in fractions of a second.

"Now," said Faldra. "Time to go places you don't know."

"How do I do that?" said Dylan.

"Find someone that does know," Faldra replied. "Go to the cafeteria."

Dylan picked up on what she was talking about. He didn't know where the cafeteria was, but could find it by melding with Faldra's presence in the Stream. In two seconds, he appeared in the cafeteria, to the mild consternation of a number of nearby people having snacks. In four more seconds—long enough to recognize that he'd gone where he was supposed to go—he reappeared in the activity room next to Faldra.

"Cool," said Dylan. "But people looked a bit irritated at me."

"Well," said Faldra, "that's because we try not to use the Stream in the course of our regular travels around the building. People would be popping all over, crashing into each other by appearing in front of someone else, that sort of thing."

"Ah, right. Makes sense."

Faldra smiled, and Dylan was freshly disarmed. "But don't worry," she said, "this time was for a good cause. No one will hold it against you."

"And now that you can do that," Faldra continued, "you can do that same thing over billions of light years. Let's have you do it over a larger distance. The thing for you to remember is that distance changes nothing in the Stream. You may think it's harder, but it's exactly the same thing. I'm thinking of a place. Take us there."

"Move both of us?" said Dylan.

"Yes."

"Right now?"

"Sure," Faldra said.

They were standing in an endless, flat field of golden plants. They looked like grain stalks, but were only up to Dylan's calf. The field went on and on all around them, on all sides, to the horizon. The sun was low. The sky opposite the sun was filled with menacing storm clouds, and the contrast of the expanse of bright grain against the near-black backdrop was an impressive sight. There was a cool breeze carrying the type of scent announcing you're about to get soaking wet.

Dylan surveyed it all silently, then spoke with an air of wonder in his voice. "Amazing. Where are we?"

"It's something, isn't it?" said Faldra. "These are the Maraba Grain Fields. They cover fifty-five percent of the planet. Not all this flat or growing this grain, but they feed billions of people in this galaxy."

Dylan stood quietly again and took everything in for a moment.

"So how far did we travel?" he said.

"This is about, oh, fifty-six trillion light years from where we were," Faldra answered.

"Oh my God," Dylan said.

"Yeah. Piece of cake for somebody bonded to the Holitaph, right?" Faldra said with a wink of one of those gorgeous eyes. "Go ahead and take us back."

"Sure," said a grinning Dylan.

In an instant, they appeared in the activity room again. Kerlan was there. "Oh! There you are," he said. "Doctor Habian, we have it. We have the serum!"

"Come on!" Faldra said to Dylan, rushing for the door behind Kerlan. They hurried back to the exam room where Urbor was.

As soon as they were in the room, Dylan asked, "Doctor Habian! Is Urbor still alive?"

"Yes, barely. Kerlan and the rest of the staff are the finest I've ever known. If there is any chance of saving Urbor's life, it will be in this," Habian said as he lifted a syringe of orange liquid. "Let's see, shall we?"

He stuck the syringe in Urbor's shoulder and smoothly administered the serum.

"Even if this saves his life," said Habian, "we need to keep our fingers crossed that the daubitira did not create permanent damage to the polydyx or other organs, or his ability to process oxygen. So few beings have ever lived through daubitira that we don't know much about how a survivor's system behaves."

"We should know if it's having some kind of effect pretty quickly," said Faldra. "If his vital signs improve at all, it's doing something. How far they'll improve or how long that will take is anyone's guess."

"Doctor," said Kerlan, pointing to a device in his hand.

"Yes, look at this. Brain wave activity is increasing and heart rate is rising."

"Wonderful!" said Habian. "Let's hope we're not too late for a good recovery."

Too anxious to go anywhere, they all stayed in the examination room to monitor every moment of Urbor's improved condition. They decided they'd be better off if they had more of Dylan's blood, so Kerlan took another two vials. They also ran a couple of innocuous tests to observe other things about human anatomy.

The tone was upbeat throughout, as Faldra and the doctors also discussed some of the characteristics of their species, for Dylan's benefit. They were a being known as Paroquin, and their planet was Hervadapalet. They existed in only six dimensions, but one was the rare Stream of Consciousness. It was one of the planets with abundant water, and plant and animal life on Hervadapalet seemed similar to Earth. There were slithering things, crawling things, and walking things. There were climbing things, swimming things, and flying things. With an atmosphere and geologic resource base similar to Earth, the two planets really couldn't develop a lot differently. All except for that missing polydyx organ in humans, which fascinated Doctor Habian to no end.

They also discussed some strategy for how Dylan could be able to free Freddie from the Galderinx ship. The Galderinx were not in the Stream, which made them a curious choice for Merdal to form an alliance. Most likely, Merdal was counting on the benefits of them not being as easy to locate, and also being a less formidable foe should relations get strained. Once Merdal had the Holitaph and could do what he wanted, he didn't seem the type to share the wealth. He would brush any helpers out of the way, and a race of creatures not in the Stream would be far easier to leave in his dust.

That left the problem of what Dylan should do once he got to the ship Freddie was on.

Locating it was easy—he had Merdal's invitation to find him in the Stream and go there. Of course, whether or not Merdal would actually be on the ship with Freddie was a question. He could be somewhere else he wanted to lure Dylan to. But Merdal would know that Dylan could also instantly leave if the situation was not what he expected, so the likelihood was that Merdal was on the ship where Freddie languished in the dallinite bubble, and was waiting to kill Dylan himself.

In fact, the question of just how Merdal would try to kill Dylan was also subject to some speculation. Dylan could not be struck by projectiles, which included the lightning energy balls fired at him on Earth and Balytre. Merdal had obviously attempted disease as a murder weapon, an ingenious approach that should, by all accounts, have worked if not for human biology.

Understanding what methods were at Merdal's disposal could help a lot in preparing Dylan for the impending rescue mission, so he quickly recounted all the recent close calls he'd had and how Freddie protected him. Besides lightning balls, those included a falling building, which was unlikely to be reproduced on a Galderinx ship, and some kind of wave that made the sky above him look bleary, like heat distortion.

That raised some eyebrows, and through some more discussion they decided it could only be a rahoga wave. Weapons that could produce a rahoga wave were not all that common, and firing one inside a ship flying in open space would normally be suicidal. Sure it would kill its target without a projectile, but would also basically rip the ship apart, killing everyone. That could work exactly as Merdal preferred: kill Dylan, dispose of a bunch of expendable Galderinx, and strand Freddie in space inside a dallinite bubble he apparently can't open, where no one can use the Stream to find him.

As far as freeing Freddie was concerned, they were going to have to bank on the notion that Merdal and the Galderinx had done a simple job of reverse engineering the hatch control and moving it to the outside. They had no way to know.

Urbor moved and opened his eyes.

Everyone rushed to him, elated, asking constant questions about how he was feeling. No one knew what a recovering daubitira patient needed, besides maybe more oxygen, but he was already wearing an oxygen mask. He was disoriented, but knew basic things like people's names and where he was. He was also wondering why he was alive, and they briefly explained about Dylan's contribution of antibodies. For the moment, Urbor was content to relax on the exam table for a bit.

Within just a minute or two, that changed. Urbor was already getting restless, pulling at things that were stuck to him. Everyone was trying to keep him calm and resting, but Urbor was quickly becoming adamant that he was alert and his ship needed him. He was insisting, and it was difficult to argue.

"How much serum is there?" said Urbor, rising off the table to his feet.

Anticipating this, Kerlan was already there with a box with twenty filled syringes. "This is it so far," he said.

"That is not enough," Urbor protested.

"You can wait until we make more," said Doctor Habian. "Or you can spread out the injections with less than a full syringe. Nobody knows what an effective dose is."

"I will take what is here," Urbor said. He took a step to Dylan. "I owe you a tremendous debt."

"No, sir," said Dylan. "I just didn't have a polydyx. Could have been anybody."

"But it was you," Urbor said. "And without you here, I would be dead."

"Not hardly," Dylan insisted. "Without me here, there'd have been no daubitira on your ship. Just take it and go save your crew."

"And you?"

"I'm going after Freddie," said Dylan.

"So be it," said Urbor. He put a furry hand on Dylan's shoulder. "Burba kikik, my friend."

"Burba kikik, Urbor," Dylan replied.

Urbor vanished. Dylan still wasn't quite used to people coming and going that way, and was momentarily startled as well as curious where Urbor had gone, since he couldn't go straight to the Zafago with its dallinite shielding. There were windows in the double doors to the lab, and from where Dylan was standing he could actually see all the way down the conveyor corridor and out the landing dock doors. Urbor's utility ship was moving away, and Dylan realized Urbor had simply transported down the hall and out to the ship. Then, once he was clear of the landing dock area of the lab building, he could zap himself and the ship back to just outside a Zafago dock door, reversing the trip they'd made to Doctor Habian's facility.

Dylan sighed. "Well," he said. "I guess I'm off, then."

Faldra stepped up to him. "Do you know what you're going to do?"

"Sure," Dylan said. "Dodge the Galderinx, don't be around when a rahoga wave goes off, and open the dallinite bubble. As soon as it's open, we're out of there."

"And then?" said Faldra.

"Back to Urbor's ship," Dylan said. "We need to help there as best we can, and there's a lot to be done. Something about the Arbar, the Studepron, and some unlo."

"Please be careful," said Faldra. "The Galderinx are a disgusting race. And Merdal...just...be careful. And remember, if you are in open space, exhale. It will buy you precious seconds." She quickly tiptoed and kissed him on the cheek. "Burba kikik, Dylan."

That may have provided all the focus he needed. "Thank you," said Dylan. He called over to Doctor Habian. "See ya, Doc."

"Take care, young man," Habian replied.

"Where's Kerlan?" said Dylan.

"He's working on more serum," said Faldra. "This will change medicine all over the universe."

"Don't hear that every day," Dylan said. He was keeping his manner light, but he was scared. This wasn't like anything he'd ever done, and the stakes were as high as they could possibly be. He was trying not to focus on that. Just roll with it, like he'd been doing. Be the hero in that movie. Make it happen however it needs to.

He let his consciousness wander until he found Merdal in the Stream. He looked squarely into Faldra's amazing eyes and said, "See you later, beautiful."

He vanished.

# CHAPTER 12

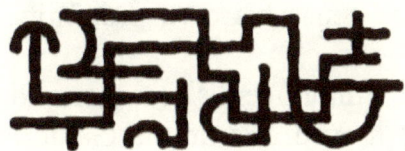

Everything around Dylan was dark, grey, and wet. Upkeep on a Galderinx ship was not a high priority. He was standing on a metal grate in a short corridor, near a corner to another corridor. Lighting was sparse, provided by shoulder-high fixtures on the metal corridor walls, at intervals of ten feet.

He peeked around the corner, as carefully to not be seen as he could.

Fifty feet down the adjoining corridor was a larger area, looking like it might be round, like a corridor hub. Off to one side, he saw the curved edge of the dallinite pod. In front of it, two Galderinx, holding weapons. Faldra was right. Disgusting. From the other side, Dylan could see two waving tentacles that could only belong to Merdal. This was the place, all right.

He took a deep breath, and had to suppress a cough. The stench on this ship was revolting.

All Dylan really had to do was get close enough to the dallinite pod to see what the Galderinx had done with the controls, with enough time to push the right button, and push it after he lured Merdal away and got him to activate the rahoga wave so the ship would be destroyed.

Piece of cake.

From Merdal's mind, he knew some of the layout of the Galderinx ship, and that the area where Freddie was held was near the center of the ship. He also knew from what Freddie told him that his bond with the Holitaph would delay Merdal's ability to sense his own proximity. That could be critical.

It was time to announce his presence and get this show on the road. Dylan moved one of the Galderinx weapons into his hands, peeked around the corner again, and fired it down the corridor, intentionally off center. The energy bolt struck one of the light fixtures in a flash of sparks.

There would be no cat and mouse maneuvering with Merdal.

He immediately produced a rahoga wave from a device he was holding, and it came quickly down the corridor, twisting and ripping all material in its path. Dylan had only a fraction of a second to react as he and that half of the ship were being blown into space.

Dylan moved instantly to the pod, even though it was now in depressurized space, beginning to float out of the open area. Merdal was still there, risking his own injuries, predicting that was the move Dylan would make.

In a moment, Dylan identified the control buttons the Galderinx had jury-rigged for the pod, but in that same moment, Merdal wrapped a tentacle around Dylan's ankle.

The Holitaph provided some protection against projectiles, but nothing would protect him against being physically slammed against any nearby solid surfaces. Also, he had forgotten to exhale, and there was pain quickly growing in his chest.

As Merdal was beginning to fling him, Dylan moved himself to a utility closet in the opposite end of the ship, which was still mostly intact. Since it was a pretty good bet the ship wasn't operating properly, there would be no functioning system to sustain air pressure very long, but he would be OK for the time being. In motion when he transported, he slammed against some tool handles and the wall of the closet, and fell to the floor. He'd have some bruises, but nothing permanent. He exhaled and took a big breath, and the pain in his chest subsided.

Merdal had the same idea Dylan did, but Dylan could sense him in a different room. Dylan had purposely chosen a room Merdal wouldn't even fit in, and it worked. Because of the Holitaph, Merdal couldn't know exactly where Dylan was yet, and to Dylan that meant the logical thing for Merdal to do at this point was to fire another rahoga wave that destroyed the rest of the ship.

Dylan paused briefly to collect himself. He was about to transport himself into empty space again, and he knew he would only have seconds. As he exhaled, he heard the remainder of the ship tearing apart very close to him.

Dylan appeared in space, a thousand feet outside the area where the pod used to be.

Pieces of the ship were everywhere. Merdal was not. He had apparently reached his limit of risking open space and fled to safety.

Dylan looked frantically around to find the floating pod. A large chunk of the ship's hull drifted past, and on the far side of it he saw the pod.

He moved to the pod. No buttons. He was getting slightly woozy.

He had pain in his arms and hands as he reached out and rotated the pod, easily done now that they were adrift. The buttons came into view, and he began to lose consciousness as he chose one and pushed it.

Dylan came to, lying on the floor in Freddie's submerged hideaway dome. He instinctively took a quick, large breath. The pain was gone, and he felt normal. He looked around, and saw Freddie sitting in his chair with a drink.

"Freddie!" said Dylan.

"Dylan, great to see you're conscious again," said Freddie as he set his drink down. "I owe you a debt for popping that hatch."

"Are you OK?" Dylan asked.

"Me? Oh, sure," Freddie said. "I was just sitting there. It's not like I was in a vacuum or anything. Question is, how are you feeling?"

Dylan used a moment to assess his condition, and began to stand. "I think I'm good," he said. "Shouldn't I have exploded or something?"

"Nonsense," Freddie replied. "That's in Hollywood. In real life, you get about fifteen seconds before the oxygen available in the blood between your lungs and your brain is depleted and you pass out. After a minute or two, you have irreversible damage and you die."

"Oh," said Dylan, moving to his chair. That chair was already his favorite, and was now becoming quite a symbol of sanctuary to him.

"But it makes it all that more impressive that you did that thinking you would explode," Freddie continued.

"Well," Dylan said, "let's just say I figured the movie version was a bit beyond, but knew I didn't have very long." An open pop appeared in Dylan's hand.

"You must be getting more adept at using the Stream," Freddie said with a smile.

Dylan described the sequence of events after Freddie was kidnapped, beginning right with the visit by Merdal in the cave on Verwen. Then he went on about the daubitira, the time on Hervadapalet with the Habians and other Paroquin, and the situation with the Zafago and Urbor's crew.

"My goodness, you've been busy," Freddie commented. "Hope you're not tired."

"I know," said Dylan, putting his pop on the table. "We need to get to the Zafago right away."

"It's difficult to get a read on Urbor's location with the

dallinite shell," said Freddie, "but not impossible, as long as he doesn't go into stealth mode and cover the windows. Give me a few minutes."

"Wait," said Dylan, standing.

"I got it, too," said Freddie. "He must be using the exposure bubble."

Dylan grinned. "And he opened a dock door for us. Ready?"

They were near the edge of an open dock door on the Zafago, a necessary move to get through the dallinite shell and into the ship using the Stream. It was only for a scant fraction of a second, then they appeared in the observation room of the infirmary.

Freddie was still in his seated position, and rolled onto his back.

"Very funny," he said as he righted himself.

"Yeah, kind of," said Dylan.

The infirmary was busy. Lenthers were bustling around, but none were on the floor pads. This was great news, as it immediately meant there were at least some survivors. Urbor appeared.

"I am so very pleased to see the two of you," Urbor said.

"Dylan was fabulous," Freddie said. "He tried to explode himself to get me out of that pod."

"I expected no less," Urbor said, patting Dylan on the shoulder.

"What about your crew?" said Dylan. "I see some activity here, which is great."

Urbor was subdued. "We lost fifteen. I know they would gladly have given their lives to succeed in this mission, but it is a saddening toll to pay."

"Urbor, I am sorry," said Dylan.

"You are not responsible," said Urbor. "You were chosen. Merdal is the culpable party here. The best way to avenge these deaths is to defeat him."

More deaths. Dylan didn't spend a lot of time dwelling

on them, but when he did, they weighed heavily. All of them. The man in the car, the casualties in his building at work, a ship full of Galderinx, and now fifteen lenthers. He had to remind himself of the focus, and that moving forward did not diminish his mourning of all those who had perished through him because of Merdal. On the contrary, it was his duty to honor those lives by pushing ahead with the task at hand.

"What's our situation here?" asked Dylan. "Do we need to get Freddie a serum shot?"

"No," said Urbor. "Once we were recovering, and the sickness was not a concern, we were able to disinfect. The material on the rock is now inert, and the disease is not present in the ventilation system."

"Excellent," said Freddie. "Then we need to get that rock back to Balytre."

"Done," said Urbor. "We will go into stealth mode, and will be near Balytre in an hour." He left the room.

Freddie sighed, and looked at Dylan. "Whatcha wanna do?"

Dylan took a second to process the idea that they might actually have a break. "I want some more millis," he said, "and a chat about the Arbar and Studepron."

Freddie nodded. "We can do that."

"Before we do, though," said Dylan, "we need a plan here. Stealth mode can't hurt, but we know Merdal can see through the dallinite somehow."

"Yes, but he can't move us out of it," said Freddie. "Otherwise, he wouldn't have left us inside when he intercepted the two of us in the escape pod. He knew we were there, but that's all. In that sense, stealth mode is critical, because even if he sees us, he can't get us out through a window, so to speak. He can only send Galderinx ships to attack, and we're fortified well against that."

"OK, I get it," said Dylan. "So Merdal must know all that, too. What's his next move, then?"

"I expect him to be waiting for us at Balytre," Freddie

said. "Now, for the millis. Shall we?"

The two of them went to the conference room, where the Holitaph was still sitting on the table as it was when Dylan and Urbor got the news about the daubitira outbreak. They got drinks and sat.

"So," said Dylan, "what's an Arbar?"

"They go together," said Freddie. "The Arbar and the Studepron. In simpler terms, a mortar and pestle. But these are a very, very special mortar and pestle. They were fashioned by Chaldrus, another of the Ancient Guard."

"Wait," said Dylan. "A mortar and pestle? You mean like a bowl and a crunchy thing?"

"Yup. The most mystically powerful bowl and crunchy thing in existence."

"So, what's unlo?" Dylan asked.

"In all honesty, I don't know," Freddie admitted. "No one on the Panel knows any more. I only know where to go to find it. Only the Barbadan actually knows what unlo is. And that shell in your bag calls the Barbadan. When you get it, you will be the second being in the universe who knows what it is."

"Well, how do we know what it does, then?" asked Dylan.

"Oh, yeah, we know that," said Freddie. "That is, we know what to do with it. It goes inside the Arbar. You get the Arbar and Studepron together, and put in some unlo. Then Xarnicus knows the words to speak, and your bond with the Holitaph is broken. Then you can hand the Holitaph to Xarnicus with 'burba kikik,' and the bonding is established again. All done."

"Right. No problem," Dylan said. "Question. You said the rock we're hauling around shows us where the Arbar is. What about the Studepron? Aren't they together?"

"Oh, no, no," said Freddie. "They're much too powerful to keep together all the time. The Studepron is hidden, with its location known only to the Oracle of Monnizo. The location of the Arbar, as you know, is revealed by the Rock of Balytre, and unlo is known only to the Barbadan. That's the way it was established by the Ancient Guard."

"But it wasn't always that way," said Dylan. "It couldn't be."

"True," Freddie said. "None of those things, even the rock, are as old as the Ancient Guard. But they were established long ago, when the security of those items became more and more important, and the traditional knowledge of the Oracle and the Barbadan are passed down genetically. It's been hundreds of millions of generations of the Oracle, and none of them have needed to tell anyone what they know. Until now."

"I sure appreciate that you know all this stuff," said Dylan. "But I can't help wondering how? If this is all ancient, secret knowledge, why do you know?"

"That's a wise question," said Freddie. "The Panel of Xarnicus is the custodian of these secrets, and has been for many eons. The Ancient Guard provided the knowledge to the Panel when they created it, and ever since then, the Panel has continued to pass it down. There are always twenty members, and when one dies, another is nominated and chosen. They are then educated in the ways and knowledge of the Ancient Guard. No one has ever needed to act on these secrets before, but the knowledge is too valuable, and the risk too great, to allow it to drift away without passing it down from member to member."

"So why have you been telling me? Why not keep all this within the Panel?" asked Dylan.

"You are a very special case," Freddie said. "You have been yanked into this under circumstances no one could have dreamed of, and now you are bonded to the Holitaph. There is no way to not tell you."

"Well, then, it sounds like our work is cut out for us," said Dylan. "And it sounds strenuous. We should still have at least half an hour to spare before we get to Balytre. I'm going to find a lenther pad and take a nap."

"That's a great idea," said Freddie. "Besides getting the rest, it'll guarantee you're out of the Stream and safe from any mental meddling from Merdal."

"Right." There were a number of lenther pads there in the conference room, and Dylan stepped over to one. "Let me know if we hit an oracle or something," he said as he got down to relax.

"I'll be with Urbor," said Freddie, getting up to leave.

The next forty minutes went by far more quietly than any since Dylan had the Holitaph placed in his hand. Urbor and Freddie were on the bridge, and the Zafago was approaching Balytre. They decided to go out of stealth mode, to provide visual connection to whatever was going on. There had been no foreign ships detected on their way there, which surprised them. Surely Merdal would not allow this operation to go uncontested.

They moved in closer to the surface of Balytre, and soon they were nearing the area of the Tanbacks, where the rock used to be. The precise plan for using the chunk of rock they had wasn't settled yet, but it would involve using stored topographical representations of the surface of Balytre to reproduce the angle of the rock face. Something was strange, though. They were still at a high altitude, but could see something on the surface that was very large. That was not right.

They descended with caution. Eventually, they got close enough to detect that what looked like it may have been an object from the higher altitude was the opposite. It was a hole. A crater. The entire area of the rock had been blasted away, presumably by Merdal. The crater was at least two miles wide and a half-mile deep.

"I think I'll go wake up Dylan," said Freddie. "Time to improvise."

# CHAPTER 13

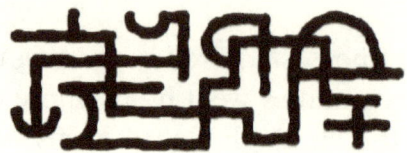

Dylan, Freddie, and Urbor stood on the bridge of the Zafago, hovering over the crater blown out of the surface of Balytre by Merdal.

"Who would do such a thing?" said Dylan.

"Someone we must thwart at any cost," Urbor said.

"What are our options?" Dylan asked. "I'm going to presume that moving a mile over is not going to help."

"That's right," Freddie said. "Without a lot of detail, suffice it to say there are particular atmospheric conditions where the rock was sitting, and the sunlight needs to filter through those exactly. We were going to try to reproduce the angle of it from three-D maps of the surface. Now there's no surface. And no time. The sun is at the proper angle very soon."

"Those maps must have the elevation pinpointed pretty well, don't they?" said Dylan.

"Yes," said Urbor. "We will use the Zafago to hover and simulate the position of the ground."

"Right," said Freddie.

Urbor gave some instructions to crew members on the

bridge, and the three of them left. First, to the conference room to retrieve the Holitaph. Then, down to the dock room where the rock was stored. When they got there, two other lenthers were waiting. One of them handed Urbor a video screen the size of a clipboard. Moments later, two more arrived with two small cranes for moving heavy items around in the cargo rooms.

Urbor moved his fingers around on the video screen he was holding, then punched a button on the panel near the door and spoke to the bridge. The topographical computer models were interpreted by the navigation system, and they were very nearly in place. He punched another button and the dock door began to open.

The lenther crew was busily wrapping straps tightly around each end of the rock. With the sun now blaring into the dock bay, they began hoisting it, then adjusting the straps to rotate the face toward the sun.

"I do not know how scientific we can be about the angle," said Urbor. "I have a visual representation, and an angle number, but I do not have a method to reproduce it quickly and exactly. I will have to estimate."

"Just do your best, as you always do," said Freddie. "Dylan, get in front with the Holitaph."

Dylan took the Holitaph in his right hand and got on one knee in front of the rock. He held it out as if it would filter the sunlight like a prism onto the face of the rock, even though at the moment all it cast was a square shadow. Freddie was off to the other side, looking intently at the rock face so as not to miss whatever information was to be shown there. In this rig, it was possible they'd only see their message for a very short time.

Urbor studied his information and told the crew on the machines to adjust a tiny bit higher.

The Holitaph began to glow, and light was passing through to the rock face. This was it!

A shadow suddenly moved down over the cargo bay,

covering the rock and the Holitaph.

"A Galderinx ship!" shouted Urbor.

A ship had indeed moved between them and the sun, several miles away. Before anyone had time to even consider something to do, the ship fired an energy beam directly at the Zafago cargo bay.

Dylan was still holding the Holitaph where he had it out in front of the rock surface. The Holitaph became very bright, with a sort of spherical halo around it. The halo deflected the energy beam precisely back to the source, and the Galderinx ship blew up in a spectacular explosion.

The entire encounter lasted eight seconds.

"Oh my God! Did you see that?" said Dylan.

No one answered, as the sun was immediately available again, and the Holitaph, still in Dylan's hand, filtered the light into a brilliant display of artwork shining brightly on the face of the rock.

"Holy crap!" yelled Dylan. "Freddie, are you getting this?"

"You bet," said Freddie.

"As am I," said Urbor, holding up his video screen.

The Holitaph went dark, and the rock face returned to having only a square shadow on it.

"Well, that was interesting," said Freddie.

"Wow!" said Dylan.

"Urbor," Freddie continued, "can you tell me any reason why your systems would not have been alerted to the presence of that ship?"

"Only if Merdal has new sorcery at his disposal," said Urbor.

"Looks like he does," said Freddie.

"Did you see that?" said Dylan. "The Holitaph just took their beam and fired it right back!"

"Quite impressive," Urbor said.

"And I could feel it inside," said Dylan. "It was like I knew what it was doing. That was totally awesome!"

"It certainly was," Freddie said, "and I'm pretty impressed with what the Holitaph continues to show us. But I'm also pretty concerned with the new things we continue to learn about Merdal. We have not a moment to lose." He moved close to the opening in the side of the ship. "Step to the opening here so I can move us."

Dylan stood up and took the couple of steps to the edge of the open dock door. "OK."

"Be careful," said Freddie. "It's slippery."

They were in an enormous subterranean cavern. Standing near one end of it, they could see that it was a good half mile long and a hundred feet high. The floor was made up of huge, smooth rocks dotted with ten-foot stalagmites, and the ceiling was adorned with numerous stalactites thirty to forty feet long. There were various places on the rock walls where water—or a similar fluid—trickled down. Dylan could see all of this because of a light green luminescent coating on many of the rocks, which Dylan took to be some type of algae or equivalent.

"You must get sick of this," said Dylan, "but where are we now?"

"You know how the undersea dome is my little sanctuary?" said Freddie.

"Sure."

"Think of this place as Chaldrus' version of the same thing."

"Chaldrus, the Ancient Guard?" asked Dylan.

"Yup."

"We're in his hideaway?"

"Yes, we are," said Freddie. "This planet is many times older than Earth."

"So we're...underwater?" said Dylan.

"Very good," said Freddie. "Yes again."

"Isn't he going to get mad that we're here or anything?" Dylan said.

"On the contrary," said Freddie. "It's essential that we

are here, and Chaldrus knows it as well if not better than anyone."

"And the Arbar is here?" asked Dylan.

"Well, you're nothing but questions," said Freddie.

"Sorry, but what else am I going to do?" Dylan said.

Freddie chuckled. "True. And yes, the Arbar is here. And being that this is probably the safest place we've ever been, it's a shame that it's so...dank. But we should just get what we came for and move along. It should be very close. Watch your step."

Dylan was looking around, but didn't know for what. "Sorry for another question, but am I really looking for a bowl just sitting around here?"

"Could be in a container, I guess," said Freddie.

"But not some special, mystical container like the Breadbox of Bananaland," Dylan said.

"Nope. Just look for something that isn't green, slimy rock."

"Right." Dylan began moving around a little, taking short steps. He slipped a little here and there, but didn't lose his balance, and didn't see anything unusual.

They wandered around silently for ten minutes, looking between rocks and around stalagmites, and eventually began to cover a fair amount of territory.

Freddie turned to Dylan. "This is wrong," he said. "The message on the rock was fairly specific. We should have seen it by now."

The ground shook from a tremendous, pounding thud they heard above them.

"What the hell!" said Dylan.

The thud came again, then a third time, each with a thundering reverberation that made the entire cavern quake.

"Freddie, what's going on?" yelled Dylan.

"This is terrible," Freddie said. "It has to be Merdal. This is...terrible."

At the far end of the cavern, they could see stalactites

moving. A smaller one broke from the roof and came crashing to the rocks below. Water came pouring in, and several other stalactites broke away and fell. Water was gushing in torrents, and would quickly fill the cavern. It would take a few moments to reach Dylan and Freddie, but only a few.

"Could he have gotten the Arbar?" said Dylan.

"No...I don't know," said Freddie. "Think, think, think."

"Freddie!" Dylan blurted. The water was crashing and surging across the cavern toward them. "How long has the Arbar been here?"

"Ageless ages," said Freddie.

"How long to form stalagmites?" Dylan said.

"Brilliant!" Freddie shouted. Pink flippers darted all around, smashing stalagmites to rubble, even as the rushing water swept them both off their feet. The surge hit the base of the wall of the cavern, curling up over the two of them, and they were instantly submerged.

After the initial maelstrom, Dylan was able to get his bearings enough to turn his body toward the bottom of the cavern again. Freddie was already righted and swimming slightly below him.

Through the water—perhaps even aided by it—Dylan saw a round edge of the Arbar gleaming out of a mound of broken rock. He gave his best underwater yell and pointed frantically. Freddie saw it, and it took less than two seconds for him to pulverize the rock around it.

Freddie, Dylan, and a little bit of water splashed to the ground on Balytre, not far from the crater where the Zafago was still hovering. Dylan took a couple of big breaths, and looked over at Freddie. Freddie held up the Arbar. Dylan smiled and held up the Holitaph, which he managed not to let out of his grasp.

The two of them stood up. "Ah, man," said Freddie, "Chaldrus is gonna be *pissed*."

Urbor landed the Zafago, and Freddie and Dylan went on

board. On their way up the ramp, Freddie said, "Here's a trick," and he used the Stream of Consciousness to move the water molecules and muddy dirt out of Dylan's clothing.

"Hey, pretty slick," said Dylan. "Didn't think of that."

"Trust me," said Freddie, "the first time you try it, don't do it on a rented tux."

They retired to the conference room with Urbor to plan their next move. The Arbar was sitting on the table. It was stone, a magnificent deep blue color, with swirls and veins of lighter blue that were reminiscent of marble. It was beautiful.

"Is the Studepron made of this same stuff?" asked Dylan.

"Yup," said Freddie.

"Why would Chaldrus allow this to be encased in rock?" Dylan asked. "What if we'd broken it?"

"This is much harder than the rock," said Urbor. "This is guardstone. It is not a glamorous name, but descriptive. The Ancient Guard created this stone especially to enhance its properties throughout the thirteen dimensions. It is, as you might expect, incredibly rare. I have not seen it before today."

"Nor have I," Freddie said. They were silent for a moment. "But," Freddie continued, "we better see more guardstone pretty soon."

"Right," said Dylan. "And as much as I don't want to hold us up or anything, can we get something to eat? I'm flippin' starving."

"At once," Urbor said. "You will certainly need your sustenance for the travels ahead." He touched a panel on the table. "Tilboran, our guests are in need of a meal. Would you see fit to grace us with three entarboro sandwiches, please?"

A voice came from the panel. "Sauce?"

"Something mild," said Urbor. "Catsup."

"At once, Leader," replied the voice. Urbor took his finger off the panel.

"Excuse me?" said Dylan. "Ketchup?"

"Earth is ignorant of virtually all other happenings in the

universe," said Urbor. He grinned and added, "But the universe is not entirely ignorant of Earth."

"OK, I get it," said Dylan. "Speaking of which." He looked at Freddie. "You know any lines from *The Ghost and Mr. Chicken*?"

"Oh! Not you, too!" said Freddie. Urbor chuckled.

"Oh, come on, Freddie, if I closed my eyes I'd think I was going through all this with Barney Fife," said Dylan.

"My favorite is *The Apple Dumpling Gang*," said Urbor.

Dylan laughed hard at this first and unexpected display of any sense of humor from Urbor.

"Oh, shut up," Freddie said with disdain.

"All right, fine," Dylan said. "Then tell me how we find the Studepron."

"The Oracle of Monnizo," said Urbor. "We must embark on a pilgrimage to the Oracle."

That seemed like an odd term to Dylan. "A pilgrimage?"

"Monnizo is a unique sort of place," said Freddie. "The universe is very, very large, and there are places within it that behave a little weirdly. Pockets of anomalies."

"That doesn't surprise me," said Dylan, "but why do we have to apparently encounter every single one of them?"

"What do you mean?" said Urbor.

"I mean the universe does this or that, except here, and that's where we're going. The Stream lets us do this amazing thing, except here, and that's where we are. We get to hit every exception to every rule."

"Well," said Freddie, "as I've explained earlier, nothing like this has ever happened before, so dealing with it is naturally going to take us to uncover the unique hiding places and obscure locales of the universe. That's the nature of acting on the secrets of the Ancient Guard."

"Yeah, well, sometimes the best hiding places are in plain sight," said Dylan.

"Perhaps," Freddie said, "unless the entire universe is at your disposal, as it is with the Ancient Guard. Then you might think differently."

The doors opened and another lenther entered with a tray of plates. There were three, and each held a large sandwich of white bread, with some sliced meat between. "Thank you very much, Tilboran," said Urbor.

"Of course, Leader," Tilboran said, placing the tray on the table. "Let me know immediately if there is anything else you need." He nodded at Freddie and Dylan, then Urbor, and left.

"Enjoy yourself," said Urbor. "Simple and delicious."

"What is it?" asked Dylan, sliding a plate in front of him and picking up a sandwich.

"Entarboro," said Urbor, also grabbing a sandwich.

"Think wildebeest," Freddie said through his first bite, "only three times the size."

"This is terrific," said Dylan with his mouth also full.

"It pleases me to hear it," said Urbor. "It is a plentiful meat. Not nearly as expensive as all that millis." He laughed.

Dylan let his own snickering subside, then decided to get back to the matter at hand. "So Monnizo is an anomaly in the universe. What kind of anomaly?"

"Monnizo itself is a planet," Freddie continued, "but it is within a solar system of twelve planets, and the entire solar system exists outside the Stream of Consciousness."

"That's not so weird," said Dylan, taking another bite of his sandwich.

"There's more to it," Freddie said. "The Stream isn't the only dimension that behaves differently there. My multidimensionality is why I can do what I do with my arms. On Monnizo, I exist in fewer dimensions. My arms are nothing more than brown, furry stumps."

"Really?" said Dylan. "Sounds intriguing."

"Maybe, but the bottom line is I'm not really any good to us there," Freddie said. "The good news is that Merdal's no good there, either. Not only can he not use the Stream, but his sorcery is ineffective. He won't be able to find you, and if he did, he wouldn't be able to do anything about it, unless he wanted to engage you in physical battle. Not likely."

"The Stream doesn't work at all?" said Dylan.

"Well, technically," said Freddie, "it's just drastically reduced. If someone is within about ten feet of you, the Stream can still connect you, but it's weak. You can't move anything. Useless."

"That does sound like a good hiding place," Dylan said. "If it's so benign, why haven't we been taking refuge there all along?"

"Yes, there's a different element of security there," said Freddie, "but also sacrifice, and I've been unwilling to trade my own abilities for that security. We can't even travel all the way there by Stream. You'll have to take a ship."

"I will accompany you," said Urbor. "Those who have made the pilgrimage say it can be grueling."

"Yeah, what is that?" said Dylan. "What pilgrimage?"

"The Oracle demands a commitment," said Urbor. "The Oracle knows the location of the Studepron, but gives guidance to many, in other matters. All make the pilgrimage."

"The Oracle lives in a crater at the peak of a mountain," said Freddie. Dylan rolled his eyes. "I know, it's cliché, but what can I say? That's where she lives, and anybody with a query for the Oracle must make the pilgrimage up the mountain, on foot, from her home village at the bottom to the peak."

"Seriously?" said Dylan. "Climbing the mountain to ask the guru for the meaning of life at the top?"

"Understood," Urbor said, "but do not take this lightly. It is the pilgrimage each Oracle makes when she ascends to the position, and it is the pilgrimage she requires of all petitioners."

"How long does it take?" Dylan asked.

"As long as it takes," said Freddie. "A couple of days."

"What?" said Dylan, then caught himself, realizing there was no changing it, and no point complaining. Besides, it

actually sounded like a great change of pace.  "So be it, then,"
he said, pushing away his empty plate.  "Got my hiking shoes
on.  When do we leave?"

# CHAPTER 14

Urbor and Dylan were a very, very long way from anywhere either of them had ever been.

They both had packs with food, water, bedding, and a few other supplies as they landed on Monnizo in the small utility ship from the Zafago, the same one they used to travel to Doctor Habian's planet. They were a short distance outside the village where the Oracles were born, from which they made their ascent to the top of Mount Majuri.

Dylan and Urbor hiked through the village, mostly a collection of mud brick homes. They wanted the ship to be near the village, in case of a need for supplies or emergency communication or anything else, but there was no reason to stop there at the moment, so they continued out of the village on the path to the mountain.

The base of Mount Majuri was roughly ten miles from the village, and it was a solitary peak, not part of a group or range of mountains. It was a lot like someone just took a mountain and plopped it down in the middle of nowhere.

Around the village was mostly grassland. As they hiked away from the village, there was a huge pasture with groups of grazing cattle of some kind. Toward the distance, Dylan could see a few small rolling hills, then larger ones, then the path got steeper as it ascended the mountain. Nearer to the base of the mountain, the vegetation changed to short trees, then taller ones up the higher hills and the mountainside.

It was warm, but the sky was overcast, and the two of them took that as a good sign to prevent overheating. Although the Oracle did assist what would be considered many petitioners, they nevertheless did not typically arrive at a rate of more than two or three each year. Making the pilgrimage to the Oracle wasn't a tourist destination. Urbor and Dylan would have the path to themselves.

Dylan had secured some ginger ale before the trip, which he nursed in small sips, and water for later, when the trek might get more dehydrating. It was not yet strenuous as they made a steady pace through the pastureland. They discussed the life of lenthers, and the life of humans, and took regular short breaks to rest for the mountainside climb.

Urbor had many interesting insights to share about the Stream of Consciousness. Lenthers were five-dimensioned beings—three spatial dimensions, time, and the Stream, exactly like Dylan. Life expectancy for a lenther was the equivalent of two hundred years, and Urbor noted that, in general, the more dimensions you existed in, the longer lifespan you had. He'd also observed that beings in many dimensions tended to develop less technology and rely on it less. The Panel of Xarnicus chose Urbor for a number of reasons, but one was that the Panel usually preferred to have at least one five-dimensioned member, and lenthers were among the most technologically advanced of those. Others in Freddie's race, for instance, would have no use for a ship like the Zafago, but the Panel recognized the value of such a resource for certain situations. Turns out their instincts were sound.

To Urbor, the Stream of Consciousness was a deeply precious and remarkable thing. It was rare, but Urbor reminded Dylan that rareness is relative. There were tens of thousands of species in the Stream, which afforded an amazing pool of shared awareness, but considering the vastness of the universe and the creatures in it, that was still an infinitesimal percentage of the beings in existence. With that perspective, existing in the Stream was an amazing priviledge.

They were three hours into the trip, and had crossed a few of the short hills.

Urbor stopped. "Listen," he said.

Dylan stopped as well, and looked around. He heard a low rumbling. He looked up, thinking it might be thunder, but the sky had not changed, and the clouds were not thick enough to be threatening. The sound got louder.

Over a hill to their left, Urbor saw some dust rising. "I do not like this," he said.

In the next few seconds, they saw the heads of a huge wave of cattle rise over the ridge. They were crazed, rhythmically pulsating heads with long, sharp horns pointing forward.

"Oh, my God," said Dylan. "Stampede!"

The herd was enormous, covering a huge path in which they were dead center. There were thousands.

"You cannot outrun them," said Urbor, "but I can. Get on my back."

"Ride you?" said Dylan.

"There is no time. Do it!"

Dylan swung a leg over Urbor's back. "Hang on to my pack," Urbor said. They both had their packs on their backs, slung over their shoulders and chests, and it was indeed the best chance Dylan had to hang on.

Urbor took off at a dead run in the same direction as the cattle. With Dylan on his back, it took some time for him to build up speed, and the stampede bore down on them relentlessly. The roar of the hooves became deafening as the lead line came up behind them. Urbor was trying to slowly drift toward the mountain, to work his way to the edge of the herd while keeping pace with them as best he could.

The cattle were faster than Urbor. Slowly, they overtook him, and Urbor and Dylan found themselves between the animals, heads and horns bobbing and weaving around them. At a desperate sprint, Urbor managed to find opportunities to weave through the dust and thundering animals toward the edge of the herd. Dylan could see the thinner outer area of the stampede.

"Almost there!" Dylan yelled into Urbor's ear.

Urbor weaved between some more of the running beasts. He was tiring.

A waving horn caught Dylan's pack and flung him up in the air.

As he was landing on the ground, he saw a log lying directly ahead of him and made a desperate lunge to get over it. He landed with his hands covering his head, and stayed that way as dozens and dozens of hooves pounded the ground all around him. Some were kicking the log as cattle jumped over it.

Slowly, the bedlam let up, then eventually dissipated into the distance as the herd moved along into the neighboring hills. The moment it seemed safe, Dylan got up to go find Urbor. He ran the same direction the cattle were running, looking for any sign. He tried to predict what Urbor would have done, working his way closer to the mountain.

"Urbor!" called Dylan as he began frantically weaving left and right to cover as much ground as he could. At the rate they were running, Urbor could have gone a long way. But he was beginning to slow down. He may not have lasted until he was clear of the herd.

Dylan ran another half mile, calling for Urbor and angling closer to the short trees that skirted the mountainside. He was panting and heaving as he saw something approaching through the shadow of a group of trees. With renewed energy, he ran to it as fast as he could. It was Urbor, lumbering weakly toward him. Dylan waved. Urbor seemed to recognize him, then he flopped flat on the ground.

"Urbor!" he yelled yet again as he got closer.

Urbor raised a hand. "I am all right," he said. Dylan stumbled up next to him and collapsed in the cool grass.

"You made it," said Dylan.

"As did you, I see," replied Urbor.

Dylan was spent, and breathing heavily. "Not sure about that, yet."

They both took a few more moments to begin to calm down. "It may not be obvious to you," said Urbor, "but it has been, shall we say, some time since I have needed to execute a sustained sprint like that."

"Me, too," said Dylan, "but I'm guessing that *is* obvious to you." He took another deep breath. "So much for saving ourselves for the mountain slopes."

They rested for several more minutes, and drank some fluids, as much as they dared. When they decided they'd recovered, they got up and started back toward the path. They were a long way off course. They tried to figure out how to angle themselves up the hills so they could meet the path a bit further along the way, but that was risky. If the path curved away from them, and they chose too great an angle, they could miss it altogether. After two miles of backtracking, they saw the path again, breathing a sigh of relief but disappointed in how much time they lost.

The next few hours were a steady trudge up the sloping base of the mountain. They stopped for a snack, complained about sore muscles from the stampede chase, and spoke about places and things Urbor had seen.

Urbor was not always on the Zafago. He spent periods back on the lenther home planet, Pra, to help maintain and advance the culture there, and especially to sire offspring. It was important to carry on the genetics that made Urbor a leader. Dylan joked about how long it had been since he'd done any "siring," and Urbor offered to take him to Pra to see what a lenther/human mix might produce, but Dylan respectfully declined.

The evening was uneventful. The path had gotten significantly steeper, and they pushed as far as they felt they could. They estimated they were over halfway, which was their goal, as they wanted to make the summit in one more day, and it would be a day of steeper climbing. They found an area off the path that was flat enough to drop a sleeping pad, and bedded down for the night.

Up with the sun, they felt refreshed and energized for the long hike. The path was mostly rocky, sometimes like steps up slabs of slate. They had been in the taller trees for some time, and they looked similar to pines or evergreens, like cedar. The path had also wound its way to the outside perimeter of the mountain. For a while, it went left and right, ambling directly up one side of the mountain, but was now more like a wide ledge circling around the mountain, spiraling up to the Oracle. There were many places where the view was stupendous, and places where the rock wall on their left was a vertical face, the same as the vertical drop-off to their right.

They were in one such place, noticing a small cave—more like an indentation—in the rock wall, when an incredible blast boomed from the mountain above them. Right away, they saw that huge chunks of rock were breaking away from the mountain face.

They quickly ducked into the tiny cave.

"What on Earth was that?" said Dylan as they watched some pieces of rock carom off the path in front of them.

"I think I know," Urbor replied, "and if I am correct, this is not good."

"Do we need to make a run for it?" said Dylan.

"To where?" said Urbor.

"Back down the mountain."

"There is no time," Urbor said.

Just then an enormous boulder thundered down and landed immediately outside, closing off a large portion of the opening to their shelter.

"Good lord!" yelled Dylan.

The ground was shaking as more large rocks bounced and tumbled down the mountain. Some smaller ones hit the boulder and bounced into their tiny cave.

"Throw them back out!" said Urbor. "We do not want those collecting in here."

Fortunately, they were not coming in faster than the two of them could hoist them out over the boulder, but then several large rocks hit the boulder and wedged into the remaining opening. There was no longer a hole large enough to accommodate either Urbor or Dylan. The rockslide continued, and they could hear more of them piling outside. After another couple of minutes, things calmed down and went still.

"Was that an earthquake?" asked Dylan, pushing against one of the rocks covering the opening to their little sanctuary. "Or a Monnizoquake?"

"No," said Urbor. He was also pushing and feeling for a place where he might be able to shift the rocks. "Mount Majuri is a volcano," he said, "and I believe we have just experienced an eruption."

"Wow," said Dylan.

"It is an awesome display of nature," Urbor said, "but a disturbing turn of events."

"Um, yeah," Dylan said. "So far, I can't even come close to moving these stones."

"Nor can I, but that was not my meaning."

"What, then?" said Dylan.

Urbor stopped pushing for a moment. "The eruption of Mount Majuri signals a succession in the Oracle."

"Oh my God! The Oracle!" said Dylan, realizing that a volcanic eruption that could move rocks the size of those blocking their cave must have obliterated the Oracle's place at the peak.

"The Oracle lives in the crater of the volcano," said

Urbor. "Sometimes the volcano erupts after twenty years, sometimes eighty, but no Oracle dies of natural causes. When it is time, the volcano erupts, and the Oracle passes to the next, down in the village. When the crater cools, the new Oracle makes her pilgrimage up the mountain."

"How long since the last eruption?" said Dylan.

"About forty-five years," said Urbor. He was fishing through his pack, and removed a short shovel. He chose a place between the rocks to wedge it and attempt to pry some space between them.

"These rocks are larger than we will be able to force apart," Urbor said.

"What do we do?" said Dylan.

"Without the Stream available, or any additional helpful aspects of other dimensions," said Urbor, "I am at a loss. I believe we can do no more than wait."

"Wait for what?" Dylan asked. There was no one on the trail, no one that could know where they were. By the time Freddie decided they were unacceptably late, and could even begin looking for them, days would pass. By the time he could actually locate them on the trail, buried under those rocks, it would be days later. Unable to use his multidimensional capabilities, it would be far longer for him to get through the rocks. If anything went wrong, they could find themselves in a tomb.

# CHAPTER 15

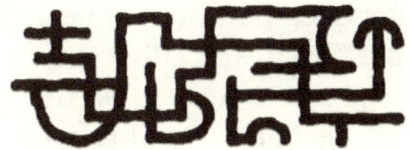

D ylan and Urbor sat in their rocky enclosure on the side of Mount Majuri and considered their situation.

"Although it is likely to be a significant amount of time," said Urbor, "at least there are people out there in the universe who know we came here and will eventually determine we have not returned."

"Just what I was thinking," said Dylan. "Somehow, I was hoping you were thinking something better than I was."

"I regret the lack of options, but it is a simple situation," Urbor said. If they angled themselves right, there was just enough room for both of them to lie down, and Urbor was already back into his pack to get out his sleeping pad. "May as well get yourself as comfortable as you can be, and have a small ration of food and drink," he said.

Dylan did as Urbor suggested, and got his bedding unrolled. The afternoon was interminable, made more so by the idea that there could be quite a few more just like it. The evening came and went as well, with spurts of conversation and long periods without. Eventually, they fell asleep.

They awoke to the sounds of tools pinging and pounding

on the rocks outside.  Dylan jumped up and began yelling, but got no response he could hear.  Then he grabbed Urbor's shovel and banged a pattern on the rock.

The same pattern came back from the outside.  Whoever it was, they knew for sure there was someone inside.  They were saved!

It took some time, perhaps an hour, but a rock rolled away from one of the upper corners of the opening.  Then another.  After a couple more, Dylan and Urbor were able to help more from inside.  The largest rock, the first one to land, was too much to tackle, but they didn't need to move it.  Both Dylan and Urbor were able to crawl over it to get outside.

Their rescuers were from the village.  They were a grey, furry, two-legged race known as Perchithods.  They were all shorter than Dylan, but thickly built and muscular.  As they began the hike back down the mountain, the Perchithods explained what had happened.  Dylan found himself very thankful that the Stream was still available even in a limited capacity, as it still allowed him to communicate with others nearby.

The Perchithods started up the mountain as soon as the initial eruption blast subsided.  There was some lava flow, but largely on the far side of the mountain, and the Perchithods knew the mountain well, including a number of short cuts from the path of the pilgrimage.  They knew precisely where Dylan and Urbor were because at the moment of the eruption, the new Oracle in the village obtained the knowledge and powers of the Oracle, and through those powers, she was aware of what had befallen the two petitioners.  She instructed the Perchithods where to go and what the situation was, so they were properly prepared to remove the tumbled rocks.

Traveling with the Perchithods back down the mountain, because of both the shortcuts and going downhill, the trip was quicker than going up, and they reached the village just before nightfall.  As they approached, there was a being standing in the village roadway. It was a large, four-legged animal with smooth skin in a mottled pattern similar to a giraffe, in green and brown. It had a short, round neck and a head with folds of skin in the jowls that reminded Dylan of a bulldog. From the head and neck flowed an impressive mane of light brown hair.

"Come, keeper of the Holitaph," the being said.

Dylan knew this was the new Oracle.

The Perchithods dispersed to other areas of the village, their job completed. Dylan walked up to the Oracle, with Urbor a few steps behind him.

The Oracle spoke again. "You are in search of the Studepron."

"Yes, Oracle," said Dylan, "but we were unable to complete the pilgrimage."

"Your trials well exceeded those of most petitioners," said the Oracle. "I will grant your petition."

"Thank you," Dylan said.

"I regret to inform you that your search for the Studepron sends you back to our Mount Majuri," said the Oracle.

"Back to the mountain?" Dylan said.

"For all of these millions of centuries," the Oracle explained, "the Oracles of Monnizo have been not simply the protectors of the knowledge of the Studepron, but of the way to the artifact itself. You will find your path to the item you seek within the molten flow at the peak of the mountain."

"Within the lava?" Dylan asked.

"Yes," said the Oracle. "The eruption of the mountain was not a coincidence with your arrival. It was necessary to make the Studepron available to you. The beacon of the Studepron has spent the life of this planet in the bowels of Mount Majuri, but now rests in the lake of molten rock at the peak."

"But if it is still in the lava, how do I retrieve it?" said Dylan.

A Perchithod approached with a box with a hinged lid,

open to reveal the contents. It was a key, but unlike any Dylan had seen, made of gold. It was large enough to grip the center section like a handle.

"When you reach the rim of the crater," said the Oracle, "hurl this key into the magma, and you will see your path to the Studepron. When you find it, the Holitaph will provide the discerning clarity you seek."

Dylan took the key and put it in his pack, startled by the weight.

"There is one more thing," said the Oracle. "The lineage of the Oracle cannot remain healthy on the basis of the DNA pool within the village. It continues through the millennia by the contributions of the petitioners who visit here. Once every generation, a petitioner is chosen to provide the DNA that is used to create the next generation. You, Dylan Bruce, the keeper of the Holitaph, have been chosen."

Dylan wanted to make sure he heard what he thought he was hearing. "Chosen to, um, contribute DNA?" he said. "What does that mean, exactly?"

"Fear not," said the Oracle, smiling. "I am not requesting that we copulate. Over the millions of generations, we have evolved to where intercourse is not required. I can reproduce based on the assimilation of some of your DNA. Here." The Oracle flipped its head and mane away from its chest and revealed a slit of an opening eight inches long. "Place your hand inside. Many cells containing your DNA will be removed from your skin, but you will not be harmed."

Although this still felt a little creepy to Dylan, he recognized that he was being honored in a tremendous way, contributing to a very long line of DNA in the genetics of the Oracles of Monnizo. His human DNA would become a permanent part of their lineage, and that was truly amazing to him.

"I accept," Dylan said. He stepped forward, extended his hand, and inserted it in the opening. It was warm and soft, but not slimy or disgusting, and she was right, he felt no pain.

"That is sufficient," said the Oracle. Dylan removed his hand. "Our thanks to you for continuing the genetic heritage of the Oracle. In six months, while the mountain cools, I will give birth, and then I will make my pilgrimage. You have done us an honor, Dylan Bruce. Continue on your quest."

"Is there anything else you can tell me about what lies ahead?" said Dylan.

"No," said the Oracle, "I have done what I am able. The Studepron is the extent of my involvement and awareness. You have our thanks for what you undertake. Burba kikik." With that, the Oracle turned and walked into a nearby building.

Dylan turned to Urbor with a huge grin on his face. "Wow!" Dylan said. He was genuinely awed by the continued experiences of this adventure, leaving his mark in the universe through things like the hereditary lineage of the Oracles of Monnizo, or a serum to recover from daubitira.

"I am impressed," said Urbor. "You should rightly feel deeply honored to be included in the genetics of the Oracles."

Dylan nodded thoughtfully, then looked up. "Well," he said with a shrug. "Back up the mountain?"

"Back up the mountain," said Urbor.

There was a place in the village for petitioners to stay for the night before they began their pilgrimage, and Dylan and Urbor bedded there. In the morning, they were out early, making it into the hilly trees without the excitement of a stampede this time. Dylan wasn't positive about remembering the shortcuts of the Perchithods and reproducing them in the opposite direction, but Urbor was more confident, so they decided to take them. This time up the mountain, it wasn't about satisfying the Oracle with a pilgrimage.

The shortcuts did mean the way was sometimes steeper. The path cut across the mountain face where the shortcuts went straight up, which meant the pilgrimage path was longer, but also took a flatter, ambling route in some areas. It also meant the shortcut routes were through undisturbed mountain terrain, with old evergreen vegetation and brush, and loose topsoil. That made it more dangerous.

It was also more ominous that the sky was darker that day, and getting progressively worse. Not long after they had progressed into some of the taller trees, it began to rain. Urbor and Dylan decided it was probably a major system coming in, because the rain increased steadily, as did the winds. There was no shelter for them, so there was nothing to do but forge ahead, but it made for rough going, with slick footing.

The winds continued to pick up and the rain remained very heavy for more than an hour.

At one point, they heard a tree cracking and coming down in the distance. A few minutes later, there was a strange noise above them on the mountain.

"Get on my back again," Urbor said urgently.

"What for?" said Dylan.

"Mudslide," said Urbor.

Dylan wasn't sure just what Urbor had in mind, but he wasn't arguing. He slung a leg over Urbor's back and held on. Urbor was considerably better and faster at climbing trees than Dylan. He chose one of the larger trees nearby and nimbly took them fifteen feet up, to where there was a branch Dylan could climb onto.

They looked down as the tree shook and almost made Dylan lose his grip. There was a huge river of muck moving down the mountain below them.

It got deeper and deeper until Dylan thought they might need to climb higher, but it receded again as the mud wave flowed further down. It was fortunate that it wasn't sliding any faster, or it would probably have wiped the trees with it, but most of them stayed put.

When the slide passed, Dylan and Urbor were faced with another problem. The ground was now covered with a foot of slime, and there was no way they were going to be able to just climb down and continue their ascent. They'd likely slide halfway back down the mountain. Urbor was not as worried about himself as Dylan, but that didn't help Dylan any.

The trees were close enough that the branches did sometimes intertwine for a portion of their height. Urbor proposed that they attempt to traverse the trees to the edge of the mudslide. This was going to prove tricky. Even though the branches intertwined, they were not thick enough to support even Dylan, much less Urbor, for simply climbing from one tree to another.

They decided to go as high as they could within the intertwining branches, then Urbor would swing Dylan as far and hard as he could so Dylan could grab a branch in the neighboring tree. Dylan would never be able to help catch the larger Urbor, so it would be up to Urbor to rush as best he could toward the end of the branches and trust that his momentum would carry him into the next tree's branches before he hit the ground.

They headed up higher in the tree they were in, and gave it a go. They worked their way out on a branch as far as it felt safe, then Dylan swung from one of Urbor's arms, back and forth until he was at maximum arc. Urbor flung him into the branches of the tree next door, and Dylan was able to grab hold of one before he began to fall. Urbor then rushed as fast as he could until the branch he was on began to droop too far, and gave a push. He did begin to fall farther than Dylan, but his lateral movement eventually carried him into the next tree's branches, and his catlike movements and instincts helped him latch on before he injured himself. The whole thing worked as closely to the plan as they could have hoped.

Now they just needed to do it again about five times until they were outside the path of the mudslide. It worked very similarly on the next two, but on the third one, Urbor was unable to get a good grip. He slowed himself down some, but couldn't latch on for good before he landed on the ground. He immediately began to slide around in the fresh mud, but managed to grab a tree trunk thirty feet down the mountainside.

Dylan was helpless to move himself between the trees, so it was up to Urbor to climb the tree he was at and work his way between them back to the tree Dylan was in.

It was time consuming and extremely strenuous, but they did make it through several more trees, the constant rain pelting them the entire time. Dylan slipped once, but caught himself on the next branch down. As soon as they thought it looked safe for traveling on the ground, they climbed down and found their way to a flat slab of slate protruding from the brush. They decided to rest, check out their bumps and bruises, and wait there until the worst of the rain had passed.

After another half hour, they were on the move again. When they came to the pilgrimage path, they figured they'd be best off to take that the rest of the way, especially since they weren't far from where the path began to hug the outer rim of the mountain and spiral up.

They passed the tiny cave with the rock in front of it, and continued on toward the peak, happy to have made it to new territory. They lost time with the mudslide, though, and it got dark before they reached the top crater. All their stuff was completely soaked, but they still had no choice but to try to bed down.

After a wet, uncomfortable night, they awoke to sunny skies and the peak of the mountain within sight.

With renewed energy, they reached the rim quickly. As they stepped up to where the path reached the edge of the crater, they were immediately taken with the wave of heat from inside. The crater was a thousand feet across and filled with molten rock. Some was red, with cooled patches of dark grey swirling around slowly within it. Neither of them had ever seen lava.

"Awesome," said Dylan.

"An impressive sight, indeed," said Urbor.

Dylan was fishing around in his pack. "No time to dawdle, I guess," he said.

"Certainly not here, at least," said Urbor. "That heat would quickly become quite uncomfortable."

Dylan pulled the gold key out of his pack. "Let's see what happens," he said as he took it with both hands, cocked his arms back above his head, and let it fly.

# CHAPTER 16

The rim of Mount Majuri was a magnificent viewpoint. Since it was a singular volcano and not part of a mountain range, and the rim was just above the tree line, a massive amount of the surrounding hills and grasslands were visible. It was an amazing vista.

Dylan and Urbor watched as the key Dylan had just thrown over his head landed in the lava of the peak crater and quickly melted.

The liquid gold spread outwardly across the surface of the magma in an unnatural way, until it formed a slender oval shape a hundred feet long, with one end near Dylan and Urbor and the other pointing toward the center of the crater. It then made a crease down the middle, folding into the molten rock and separating it. The fold went deep into the lava, and it separated farther and farther until it was as if a pie piece had been cut and removed right out of it.

The path went down into the pie piece, forty feet deep but with a solid rock floor, and the walls were gold. Down the path, not far from the point of the wedge, Dylan and Urbor could see a shining blue object.

"Just...absolutely amazing," said Dylan.

"A spectacular phenomenon," said Urbor. "I believe that is the Studepron."

"Let's go find out," Dylan said.

They started gingerly down the path, making sure the way was cool on their feet once they were within the wedge of gold holding back the lava. Not only was the rock cool, but the golden walls were somehow protecting them from the intense heat of the molten rock. In continuous amazement at the sight, they progressed further until the lava level was above their heads.

The wedge got deeper and narrower, but still there was no heat around them or under them. As they approached the glowing blue object, though, they could see it was larger than the Studepron would be, and was not resting on the ground. It was about the size of a basketball, and even the same shape. From a few feet away, they could see it in detail. It looked like the planet Saturn, but the ball was all white and the rings were a brilliant blue, similar to the guardstone color. It was hovering four feet in the air, and slowly rotating along the plane of the rings.

Urbor was the first to state the obvious. "This is not the Studepron," he said.

"No," agreed Dylan, "but it does make sense from all the cryptic references of the Oracle."

"I noticed that, too," said Urbor. "She did not ever state with certainty that the Studepron was here."

Dylan was rummaging through his pack again. "Right. She said the 'path,' the 'way,' and the 'beacon of the Studepron' was here." He pulled the Holitaph out of his pack. "She also said the Holitaph would provide the clarity we seek."

"I recognize this," said Urbor.

"Yeah?" Dylan said. "What is it?"

"This is a representation of Ayaplune," Urbor explained. "It is a world of ice, with rings of tiny pieces of stone."

"Tiny, like the size of a pestle? And blue, like guardstone?" said Dylan as he reached out with the Holitaph toward the hovering ball.

"Precisely," said Urbor. "The makeup of the Rings of Ayaplune consists largely of lapis plunic, a stone of blue very similar to guardstone. It would be an ingenious place to hide the Studepron."

As Dylan held the Holitaph, there was a speck in the rings that sparkled like it was glimmering in the sun. Dylan pulled the Holitaph away, and the glimmering stopped. He reached it forward again, and the sparkle returned.

"Well, well," Dylan said.

"It would seem the Studepron has been placed among the billions of fragments of lapis plunic in the Rings of Ayaplune," Urbor stated.

"It would seem," echoed Dylan. Out of curiosity more than anything else, Dylan reached his hand out to touch the edge of the rings in the hovering beacon. There was no substance. His fingers went through it like a hologram. "Cool," he said.

"Intriguing," added Urbor.

"I imagine we should be on our way," said Dylan, "since we're standing next to millions of tons of magma being held up by gold walls no thicker than plating."

"Agreed," said Urbor.

They returned out of the wedge, at an awkwardly nervous pace. When they reached the top of the rim again, they turned back to the crater. The gold swirled into the molten rock, and the lava poured quickly back together.

Dylan looked at Urbor. "If I thought you knew who Moses was…"

"Save it," said Urbor. Dylan smiled at the uncharacteristic informality.

They proceeded briskly down the mountain again. The entire event at the rim took less than an hour, and they had good weather and a downhill trip ahead. Even avoiding the mudslide area, if they kept a determined pace they could spend the next night in the village.

They arrived there at the cusp of darkness, utterly spent. This time, there was no one to greet them, but they were able to bed down in the same accommodations as two nights before. It was a deep, satisfying rest.

The next morning they were back out to their utility ship for the return trip to the Zafago. It took an hour or so to travel far enough outside the solar system that they could use the Stream of Consciousness, and they moved near the Zafago as soon as they could.

Freddie seemed concerned that they'd been gone an extra two days, but not to the point where he was ready to do anything drastic. When Dylan and Urbor explained everything that happened, it was just the sort of thing Freddie figured was probably going on.

It was curious how fascinated Freddie was by the entire encounter with the Oracle, hanging on every word about the key, the beacon pointing the way to Ayaplune, Dylan's DNA contribution to the genetic legacy of the Oracles, even details as simple as what the Oracle looked like. It was obvious Freddie was more envious of the two of them than he had let on before they left. He was like a kid hearing about someone's trip to the North Pole to see Santa.

Dylan was freshly reminded that most of what they were going through was very different and exciting for Freddie and Urbor. Their experiences were things that all past members of the Panel of Xarnicus accepted as legendary knowledge but never had to act on or see in front of them, and some lived lives far longer than Freddie's million years. As outrageous as all of this was to Dylan, parts of it were no less outrageous to Freddie and Urbor. They both seemed cool and collected, but Dylan knew that was largely because there was so much they had to teach Dylan about the nature of the universe. Compared to their daily lives, in which people like Dylan weren't around being hunted by an epic sorcerer capable of destroying the fabric of the universe, this was very special stuff.

Urbor and Dylan had been subsisting on a drastically reduced level of the rations they packed, and both were starved and thirsty, so they quickly ordered up a feast. This time, something different for Dylan, a roast of something more like chicken than the entarboro sandwiches he had before. Delicious.

They planned their next move to Ayaplune. It was close enough to take the Zafago, but it would be two days. That would easily be long enough for Merdal to zero in on Dylan's location and make life difficult. They would need to move Dylan around some.

Freddie's underwater dome was a good place, of course. After the first few hours on the Zafago, Freddie took Dylan to the dome. Dylan brought along a video game from home to help pass the time. They set a schedule for Urbor to go to the exposure bubble and place himself outside the dallinite shell for a moment, so Freddie and Dylan could find the Zafago and return. They did that back and forth several times.

This worked well for the first day, and overnight was not a concern, as sleep took them out of the Stream in any event. The second day, they decided as long as they needed to send Dylan somewhere, he and Freddie should scout ahead in the utility ship and go to Ayaplune, to find out things like whether the Holitaph would truly signal the location of the Studepron the way it did in the beacon. After a breakfast designed and created by Dylan to indoctrinate Urbor and Freddie to the ways of bacon, eggs, and biscuits and gravy, Freddie and Dylan took off in the utility ship to Ayaplune.

The first impression on Dylan's mind when they appeared a hundred thousand miles off of Ayaplune was how gorgeous it was. The stark contrast of white sphere and blue rings was exceptional.

They had no idea how close to the Studepron they needed to be to interact with the Holitaph, but it became apparent that a hundred thousand miles was too far away. There was nothing in the rings that was sparkling in any noticeable way.

Freddie guided the craft in closer to the rings.

From afar, they looked very flat, but closer, it was clear they were actually many miles thick. Freddie brought the ship as close as he could while remaining safely outside the zone of floating debris, and navigated against the rotation of the planet and rings, so as to cover as much area as quickly as possible. Dylan took the Holitaph and held it in his hand, in case its effects were stronger if it was touching him.

They slowed to a speed that would require two hours to traverse the entire length of the rings. That was about as long as they figured they wanted to be out and away from the Zafago.

Somehow, it felt like a long shot. The rings were thousands of miles wide. They were going right down the middle, but it seemed like a lot of area to cover. They had no reason to expect the influence of the Holitaph to be limited to any given range; it just felt like it.

Their first sweep confirmed their suspicions. There were no indications of the Studepron glowing in the rings on their first pass. They returned to the Zafago and docked, waiting for a time there before the next pass at Ayaplune. It passed uneventfully, and Freddie and Dylan took the utility ship back to Ayaplune for another run.

This time, they moved closer to the planet, to concentrate on the inner half of the rings. The searching was tedious, but it had to be done. Another two hours went by without success.

Back to the Zafago.

After a time, back to Ayaplune for a pass at the outer half of the rings.

No luck.

By this time, the Zafago was only about three hours away from Ayaplune, and they decided to discuss a different strategy. There really wasn't anything to do but narrow the search to smaller areas, though this felt disappointingly like a needle-and-haystack scenario. Moving the utility ship closer to the rings was dangerous, and still slow in relation to their confidence that they would actually find the Studepron that way.

Urbor had a humanoid pressure suit aboard the Zafago. In spite of the time, it could be best for Dylan to take the suit and use the Stream to move among the stone fragments in the rings, pausing for a few seconds in each location to see if the Studepron was nearby. It could get tiresome, but that seemed kind of the point of hiding the Studepron there. With the Holitaph, it could still be a frustrating search, but without it, completely impossible.

The Zafago came within a comfortable range of Ayaplune, and Dylan got prepared in the pressure suit, Holitaph in hand. The suit was considerably less cumbersome than what Dylan was used to envisioning as a space suit, but it did cover his entire body, including a helmet, so movement wasn't quite as nimble as without it. For an individual, the exposure bubble on the side of the Zafago was sufficient to get outside the dallinite shell for movement in the Stream, and Dylan crawled inside it, then disappeared into the Rings of Ayaplune.

The first thing Dylan did was search briefly for a chunk of rock he knew he would recognize, as a landmark so he would know when he had traversed the entire circumference. Then he would move in closer a bit, find another distinctive rock, and begin around the rings again, mapping layer by layer, like playing a record album from the outside in. He still had no idea how close he needed to be to the Studepron to see it sparkle, but he tried to pick a distance roughly equal to the thickness of the rings. Seemed like a good method to start. He moved, scanned the rocks for signs of the Studepron, and moved ahead again.

Urbor had earlier recommended they keep the Zafago in an orbit synchronous with Dylan's movements, and it was a comfort to him that it was always visible. After he had moved himself a few dozen times, he noticed flashes of light from space. He looked out toward the Zafago.

Three Galderinx vessels were nearby, firing energy blasts at the ship. They were discovered!

# CHAPTER 17

Floating in space between the blue rock fragments of the rings of Ayaplune, Dylan's thoughts were racing.

Freddie had said earlier that the Zafago was well-defended against Galderinx attack, but three-to-one odds couldn't be good. He didn't know how much time they had.

He could go to the Zafago, using the exposure bubble to get back on board the same as he had left, but that had to be what the Galderinx—and, by extension, Merdal—were expecting, and therefore hoping. There was no reason to believe they had any idea he was not currently on board, so that plan would no doubt play into their hands.

He could go somewhere else entirely, but that would not only be abandoning the Zafago, he also would have no idea what was happening. Unacceptable. He could go aboard the Galderinx ships and wreak some havoc that way, but that was unpredictable and not a very immediate method to stop or destroy them, depending on what he found on board.

Dylan then remembered what happened on Balytre, when the Galderinx ship appeared between them and the sun, and fired into the cargo bay. The Holitaph returned the energy blast in kind.

He was holding the Holitaph in his hand.

Decision made.

Dylan moved himself a hundred feet outside the hull of the Zafago, directly in the line of fire of one of the Galderinx ships, holding the Holitaph out in front of him. It immediately became very bright, with the same halo around it that formed on Balytre.

In another few seconds, one Galderinx ship was destroyed.

Dylan moved between another Galderinx ship and the Zafago, but it had already ceased firing. Dylan immediately moved again, recognizing that even if Merdal couldn't read his position with the Stream right away, his movements were giving it away, and Merdal could move him somewhere himself, essentially kidnapping Dylan.

In theory, Merdal couldn't move Dylan. At least he had told Dylan he couldn't because of the Holitaph, but Merdal clearly could not be trusted, and in reality Merdal had already thwarted properties of dallinite and cloaked Galderinx ships from Urbor's proximity sensors. Although Freddie had never had any trouble moving Dylan, Merdal claimed he could not, because of his own peculiar relationship with the Holitaph. That could merely have been to lure Dylan into acting from a false sense of security. Regardless, it would be careless to make any assumptions about what Merdal could or could not do with Dylan.

From where Dylan was, he could see the Zafago and the remaining two Galderinx ships. After a few seconds, he moved again to another similar vantage point. He watched from there as the Galderinx vessels turned and backed away from the Zafago, then sped off into space. Dylan immediately moved on board the Zafago, into the exposure bubble, and headed for the bridge. On his way there, he ran into Freddie.

"Everybody OK?" said Dylan.

"Great thinking," Freddie said. "Yes, we're fine.

Dallinite can take a lot more of that, but there's certainly no reason to put ourselves through it if we don't have to. You sure gave Merdal something else to think about."

"Should we go somewhere else for a while?" asked Dylan.

"Not at all," said Freddie. "He won't attack again, at least not soon. On the contrary, this is probably our safest time to search."

"Right, right," said Dylan. "But if there is any kind of way for him to see my movements, I don't want them to be in too predictable a pattern."

"Yes, seems smart," said Freddie.

"I know I'm giving up the benefits of a systematic approach, but I'm going to go pretty much randomly."

Freddie nodded. "I agree."

"OK. Well, nothing to be gained by staying on board, then."

"I'll tell Urbor we chatted," said Freddie.

"Right." Dylan turned around and headed back to the exposure bubble. He climbed in and popped himself into the blue rings once again.

It was interesting to Dylan that there could be so much actual space between the rock fragments, sometimes only ten or twenty feet, but sometimes a hundred, yet the rings looked so solid from far away. He moved around wherever his curiosity took him, checking out the different shapes and sizes of rocks, always with the Holitaph in hand to locate the Studepron.

Dylan spent the next half hour moving and looking, making sure every few moves put him within sight of the Zafago, in case Merdal and the Galderinx came back.

It probably should have seemed more tedious than it did. All of this sort of thing was still far too new and astounding to Dylan for any of it to be boring. In the utility ship, just sitting there drifting along, it got dull. Out here by himself, bouncing around wherever he wanted to go, it was fun.

He'd been at it for long enough that it came as a complete

shock when he popped into one position fairly close to the inside edge of the rings, and something off to his left was glowing.

He moved over to it immediately, and it was there!

The Studepron shone brightly in front of him. Out of curiosity, he briefly let go of the Holitaph, to see if the Studepron would continue to glow from proximity, but it did not. The Holitaph only made the Studepron glow when Dylan was holding it.

Dylan grabbed both items and moved into the exposure bubble of the Zafago. One of the other lenthers was nearby, and Dylan politely asked him to call the bridge and tell Urbor he was on board. The lenther happily did so, elated that the Studepron had been found.

Urbor immediately changed the flight course of the Zafago for a destination of Rondaka, Kof's planet, where the unlo was. He then joined Freddie and Dylan in the conference room for a celebratory toast at finding the Studepron.

This was an outrageous and amazing adventure for Dylan, but for Freddie and Urbor, seeing the Arbar and Studepron, and being among the only creatures in the history of the universe to actually touch them and have them together in the same place, represented a kind of experience beyond words for them.

These were legendary mystical items created by the Ancient Guard, items revered by the Panel of Xarnicus for the length of its existence. Freddie and Urbor were incredibly happy, and grateful to Dylan for his engagement and persistence in tracking these down.

Rondaka was another day away. The energy was positive and emotions high as the Zafago made its way there. Merdal's powers were never to be underestimated, but he did seem to be limited in the available methods for tracking or attacking Dylan, as long as everyone was aboard Urbor's ship. For safety, Freddie and Dylan did some more shifts in Freddie's underwater dome, but the trip went by otherwise uneventfully.

When they arrived at Rondaka, it was during the morning hours there. The sun's circles had not lowered in the sky any appreciable amount over the days since they'd been there last. Urbor brought the Zafago down to land near the buildings Dylan had seen before, with the restaurant Kof was in, but things were drastically, terribly different.

There had been a horrible tragedy here.

All of the buildings had been blasted or burned to the ground. There was nothing but charred rubble.

This had Merdal's fingerprints.

Nothing was still smoldering; it looked like this happened a while ago, probably days earlier, right after they picked up Dylan with the Zafago. If there was anything else to ask or learn from Kofklapanvik, that opportunity had passed.

And there were things to ask.

Urbor and Freddie actually knew less about unlo than they did about either the Arbar or Studepron, which had been created by Chaldrus of the Ancient Guard and had information passed down from the Guard through the Panel of Xarnicus. Unlo was a mysterious substance no one knew by anything other than legend or prophecy. According to Freddie, even on Rondaka, the entire area of the planet where the dirt turned green had been avoided as cursed for as long as anyone knew.

In Urbor's view, it was difficult to fault anyone for that perception. He explained to Dylan that the atmospheric conditions of Rondaka created distortions and other multidimensional problems over certain parts of the planet, such that the green dirt could not even be found or confirmed from the Zafago. The only way to reach it was on the ground, and no one had tried that since before memory.

*Naturally. In all the universe, there's probably only one planet where the surface can't be seen from an airborne vessel, and that's where we have to go.*

Even the Call of the Barbadan, the shell in Dylan's

saddlebag, had been taken from Rondaka long before. Freddie regaled the group with a tale of how the shell found its way into his possession, and the twisted circumstances of time travel that resulted in Freddie delivering the shell to Kof forty-two years before Dylan got there. The Ancient Guard had to have been an integral part of that situation. It was safe to say Freddie had seen some interesting things in his million years.

Just to make certain, Dylan asked if the Stream worked on Rondaka, even though he remembered that Freddie had moved them both there from the underwater dome. Urbor and Freddie both confirmed that Rondaka's unique conditions did not render the Stream ineffective. It was merely that the legendary green dirt seemed to distort both visual and sensory observation from any appreciable distance away.

So here they were, with nothing to really go by except Kof's earlier description that Dylan should ride away from the sun until the dirt turns green, then blow the Call of the Barbadan. Dylan's earlier experience, though, showed that the rotation of the planet would result in a large circle of travel, unless there was another way to navigate, which was not apparent.

There was also one other option to discuss. Instead of traveling at a walking pace, Dylan could gallop on the parmalon, and outrun the curvature of the sun's arc. There was no telling how far it was to the green dirt, or whether the parmalon could make it without tiring out. They could fly there in the Zafago, just over the ground surface, but there was also no telling if any aspects of calling the Barbadan were contingent on making the trip overland, just as the pilgrimage on Monnizo. Mystical multidimensional influences could be at work here. If they tried to go there by air, and the call was unsuccessful, it would be that much time wasted.

And time was not to be wasted at this point.

They knew Merdal was aware of this world, and aware that part of Dylan's mission included Rondaka. He may even have known specifically about unlo. Any mistakes or delays could give Merdal the opportunity he needed.

In the end, they decided to split the difference. They would fly as far as Dylan had traveled the first time, but in a straight line, not in the curve Dylan took. From there, Dylan would gallop on the parmalon and find the place where the dirt turned green. Neither Freddie nor Urbor could accompany him here.

Urbor's crew had been taking excellent care of the parmalon, and they brought it to the hatch dock to meet with Dylan. He got packed up with the Call of the Barbadan, lots of water, and a container like a canning jar to hold some unlo. He was happy to be reunited with his hat, and unhappy to be reunited with the mask he needed to wear to survive breathing on that planet.

At least he could exist here. For both Freddie and the lenthers, elements in the atmosphere would eventually be fatal even from simple contact. Dylan wondered if the reason had something to do with a polydyx or some other organ he did or didn't have.

Dylan put his hat on and stepped around to the face of the animal. "Remember me?" The parmalon nodded in its established, seemingly random fashion. "Ready to run?" Another nod. "Let's go find some unlo, then." It nodded yet again. Dylan got up on the saddle, and signaled to Urbor.

The hatch lowered and Dylan took off down the ramp and across the desert.

The parmalon's gallop was remarkably smooth and fast. Dylan kept the sun at his back as they traveled swiftly through midday. He stopped after twenty minutes and got down off the parmalon to offer some water. The animal drank a little, but seemed fresh and anxious to run. Dylan was happy to accommodate.

After another fifteen minutes at a constant gallop, Dylan did notice that the topography was changing. They were still running on hard dirt, but there were more rocks dotting the landscape, mostly small ones, the size of a baseball or grapefruit. Soon, the rocks were more plentiful and generally larger.

Within another ten minutes, the landscape was too rocky for the parmalon to gallop. They stopped for more water, then Dylan continued riding, but at the parmalon's walking pace. Dylan was hoping they'd covered enough ground that walking wouldn't matter at this point.

It was the rocks that changed first. They got darker, then took on a greenish hue. As the dirt beneath them did the same, the rocks became a full, dark green. Kof had said "when the dirt turns green," so Dylan waited until everything underfoot was the same dark green.

He stopped and climbed down off the parmalon.

"You were magnificent," he said to the parmalon, patting its neck. The animal nodded again, and Dylan wondered what it would do if he ever said something it didn't agree with.

Dylan dug into one of the bags hanging across the parmalon's back and removed the Call of the Barbadan. He looked it over, simply admiring it more than anything, as there was only one place to blow into. He lifted up his mask, held the shell to his mouth, pointed it up in the air, and pushed as much air through it as his lungs would allow.

# CHAPTER 18

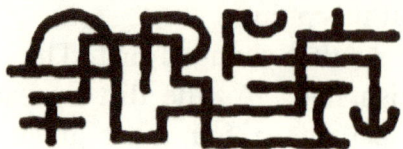

Standing next to his trusty parmalon steed within the dark green rocks and dirt of legendary uncharted Rondaka, Dylan heard absolutely nothing.

He expected to hear something when he blew through the shell, the Call of the Barbadan, but he did not. He took a deep breath through his mask, then lifted it, put the shell to his lips, and blew again.

Nothing. With everything Dylan had been through, the more he thought about this, the more it didn't really strike him as all that odd, or as a failure of any kind. He would have preferred to hear something, so he would have some idea that it was working and not plugged up or anything, but he certainly knew better than to assume it was a dud. He found a rock to sit on, and waited.

Fifteen minutes went by.

Dylan looked as closely as he could in all directions, and eventually thought he saw something moving near the horizon. It was farther in the same direction he had been traveling, away from the sun. He wondered if he would have had to wait less if he had continued traveling himself before he used the call, but somehow he didn't think so.

Dylan watched as the figure came slowly closer and closer. Eventually, he made out that it was something riding on something else, a lot like he thought he would look riding the parmalon.

In another couple of minutes, he saw that it looked exactly like him riding a parmalon.

Dylan stood still as the being approached the final few hundred feet, then stopped twenty feet away. It was a mirror copy of Dylan and the parmalon.

Dylan spoke first. "Are you the Barbadan?"

"I am," said the being, sounding like Dylan as well.

He got down from his parmalon, and walked over to Dylan. He reached up and pulled Dylan's mask off, then placed his hand gently on Dylan's neck. He moved it slowly down to Dylan's chest, then handed him the mask. Dylan knew he wouldn't need it any more. Without the mask, he could smell this planet for the first time. In the green area, at least, it smelled green. Like freshly cut grass.

"And you are Dylan Bruce, keeper of the Holitaph."

"I hear that a lot," said Dylan. He still surprised himself with his attitude in some of these situations, but it wasn't as much from confidence as that it was just all too much to really, fully grasp. Detachment was still part of the coping mechanism. He'd also come to terms with moving forward with his life, so there was an element of having nothing to lose in his new approach to living.

"And I hear that I have no sense of humor," said the Barbadan. It occurred to Dylan that the fact that he said so belied the falseness of the statement, but he made no further comment on it.

"I must ask," said Dylan. "You appear as me?"

"I do," said the Barbadan. "You would not...understand if I appeared in anything like my natural state."

"Twelve dimensions?" Dylan said.

"Ten," replied the Barbadan.

"Say no more," said Dylan.

"I should not speak?" said the Barbadan, walking back to get on his parmalon. "That might be difficult."

"It's an expression," said Dylan. "But you knew that already."

"That's true, I did," the Barbadan said as he slung a leg over his animal. "I know much about you, but try to learn more before we embark on a quest for unlo."

"Why is that?" said Dylan, moving to get back on his own parmalon. If this was a quest, there would be additional traveling.

"There is much at stake," said the Barbadan. "No one has attempted to find unlo for a very, very long time, and no one has needed it for your purpose, ever." He turned his parmalon to his left—Dylan's right—and began ambling forward. "Come with me," he said.

"So this is an incalculable thing that is happening," the Barbadan continued, "and completing your task needs an individual with certain characteristics. I am not required to reveal the unlo to just anyone who shows up with the Call."

"What sorts of characteristics?" asked Dylan.

"There's no formula," said the Barbadan in a mocking tone.

*OK, this dude is weird.*

"Sorry," the Barbadan continued, "but I occasionally attempt to relate to new species in a way that incorporates aspects of their culture into the conversation."

"And out of everything going on in my head, you picked sounding like a spoiled high school kid to assimilate?"

"I said sorry," the Barbadan echoed in the same mocking tone.

"Ah, now that was funny," said Dylan. "I knew you were lying when you said you had no sense of humor."

"But I didn't," said the Barbadan. "I said others have said I don't."

"Fair enough," said Dylan. "So, are you, like, the

protector of the unlo?"

"Not exactly," said the Barbadan. "I am simply the only one who knows what it is and how to get to it."

"I see."

"And since that is true, I have the power to help or not help."

"Right."

"Fortunately, I am keenly aware of the criticality of finding the unlo, and am therefore predisposed to help, unless you turn out to be a total douche bag."

*OK, this is just crazy. I'm having a conversation with myself, but myself is really a socially challenged weirdo entrusted with the sole knowledge of one of the most mystically powerful substances in existence.*

"Understood," said Dylan. "So what's with the shell thing? Where did that come from, and how does it call you?"

"Well, I don't have to come if I don't want to," said the Barbadan. "I'm not a slave to the thing."

"Of course not."

"But the truth is, I made it myself," the Barbadan said. "I don't have a cell phone, and sometimes people need to get in touch with me."

"I couldn't hear it," said Dylan.

"Oh, no," said the Barbadan. "It's just for me. Maybe I should make another one now with caller ID!" He chuckled. It seemed the more time he spent looking like Dylan, and being around Dylan, the more he took on human behavior and attitude, but it came out unnaturally.

Dylan didn't really want the peripheral conversation to continue any longer than it had to. It had a strange tone, and Dylan felt like he could say something wrong at any time and screw this up beyond repair. The Barbadan clearly did not spend enough time around other beings. Dylan tried to steer the subject matter to the quest at hand.

"So, this quest," said Dylan. "Where are we headed?"

"Wherever I want to go," said the Barbadan. This was

not a good sign. It sounded to Dylan like he was being toyed with. Time for a different, more direct approach.

"Is there some kind of test I need to pass?" Dylan asked. "Some douche bag litmus test?"

"In a hurry?" replied the Barbadan.

"You know I am," said Dylan. "I'm in a race, in fact. A race against Merdal to get the things we need to transfer the bonding of the Holitaph to Xarnicus, where it belongs, before he kills me. If I die, the Holitaph is up for grabs, and I have friends on board the Zafago that have gone through too much and done too much for me to watch it all slip away now."

The Barbadan pulled up and stopped. "OK," he said. "I just wanted to know this was for Xarnicus, your friends, and the fate of the universe, and not for saving your own life. I thought I could feel it in you, but now I know for sure. Get down."

Dylan got off his parmalon, and the Barbadan did the same. The terrain had not changed at all, still the dark green dirt and rocks.

The Barbadan waved his left hand in a loop over his head.

When he did so, everything around them transformed. It became a jungle, with trees, huge ground ferns, and sounds. Trickling water sounds and strange animal sounds. It still smelled of freshly cut grass, but with more, like flower scents.

Not far away, Dylan could see a large, tall rock formation rising above the jungle, with strange faces carved in it.

The Barbadan pushed aside a plant stalk and gestured to Dylan. "This way," he said.

"Is that water for real?" asked Dylan. "This poor parmalon has been run to death."

"That's where we're headed," said the Barbadan.

He led the way through the thick vegetation, and Dylan led the parmalon behind him. They came to a tiny clearing near a babbling creek about ten feet wide. The water was crystal clear and quite inviting.

"Refresh yourself," said the Barbadan.

"I'll stick to what water is left in my bag," said Dylan, "but the parmalon has earned this."

The animal put his front legs in the creek, drank, and nodded.

"From here, we go alone," said the Barbadan. "Bring your unlo jar."

Dylan pulled his jar from the bag and patted his steed's neck. "I'll be back," Dylan said to the parmalon, who nodded again.

The Barbadan gestured toward the creek water. "In the water," he said. Dylan looked puzzled. "Trust me," the Barbadan continued, "it's the safest way to travel. The small animals are...unfriendly."

Dylan stepped into the creek and followed the Barbadan at a careful, steady pace.

"Stay close," said the Barbadan, looking around with each step. Dylan did so.

After a few minutes, they came to a small lagoon at the mouth of the creek. Across the lagoon was the rock formation Dylan had been seeing above the vegetation. It was fifty feet tall, covered in carvings, with a twenty-foot cave opening in the base of it. To the left of the base of it was a small beach of white sand, a hundred feet long.

The Barbadan stopped just before the mouth of the creek. "Get down," he said, lowering himself to one knee in the water. Dylan followed suit. The Barbadan pointed to his right, down to a disgusting animal that looked like a mutant crab, moving down the bank of the creek.

"Don't let that bite you," he said.

Then he raised his arm to point across the lagoon to their right.

"Look."

Dylan was trying to divide his attention between what was across the lagoon and the mutant crab, which was making its way farther down the creek bank, away from them. Across the lagoon were three animals, drinking at the edge of the lagoon. They were the size and shape of small pigs.

"Stay down," whispered the Barbadan. From out of the cave opening shot a burst of liquid that hit one of the pig animals. It fell over limp as the other two scattered into the foliage. An enormous, grotesque creature filled the cave opening. It walked on two legs, but was covered in scales, with a huge, wide head and mouth with tusks. It looked like the incarnation of someone's nightmare.

It lumbered through the edge of the lagoon to the unconscious pig animal, picked it up, and bit it in half. It chewed a little, then tossed the rest of the animal in its mouth. Chewing some more, it turned and splashed through the lagoon across to the beach sand. It squatted there for several seconds, stood, and walked back into the cave.

"Now!" said the Barbadan, taking off and sprinting through the shallows of the lagoon off to their left. Stunned by what he had just witnessed, Dylan was caught quite by surprise, but sprang to his feet and followed. It only took fifteen seconds to run around the edge of the lagoon to the beach. Waving to Dylan, the Barbadan plunged to his knees next to a wet patch in the sand. "Quickly!" he said.

Dylan knelt alongside the Barbadan. "This?" he said.

"This is it!" said the Barbadan.

"But—"

"It's soaking in!"

Dylan put his trepidation aside and unscrewed the jar top in one motion. He plunged the jar into the soft, wet sand and got it nearly full.

"Yes! Yes! Yes!" said the Barbadan.

Dylan put the lid on the jar tightly. "This is it?"

"That, my intrepid friend, is unlo."

"This is monster pee," said Dylan, reaching the sealed jar down to the water to rinse off the wet sand on the outside.

The Barbadan was clearly beside himself at having an opportunity to explain this to someone. "That is the urine of a creature unique in the universe," he said, "combined with a sand mixture unique in the universe. These two items, and only these two, combine to form unlo."

"I can appreciate that," Dylan said, "but I hope it won't hurt your feelings too badly if I just tell my friends I got it, and not how."

The Barbadan stood up and waved his left hand in a loop over his head. The entire environment transformed again, and Dylan found himself sitting on hard, dry dirt, between several dark green rocks. He stood.

"Just save the universe," said the Barbadan. "Just do what you came to do. Burba kikik, Dylan Bruce." He waved his right hand over his head, and disappeared.

A thousand feet away, above the rocks, Dylan could see his parmalon standing alone. He took two steps in that direction when a different, more menacing monster appeared in front of him.

It was Merdal.

# CHAPTER 19

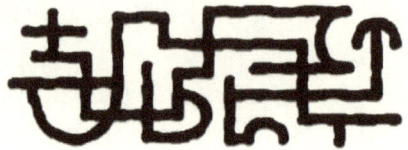

Among the green rocks of Rondaka, even with Merdal directly nearby, Dylan quickly assessed that his life was not in immediate danger here. He could go anywhere on a moment's notice. This had to just be a threatening reminder of some kind.

"So, you have all your little trinkets," Merdal said.

"Not quite," Dylan replied.

"Save your feeble breath," Merdal admonished. "I know well what you have been doing, and what you have planned. You may even believe you have made significant accomplishments."

"Just a little sightseeing," said Dylan.

"There is only one meaningful thing for you to achieve," said Merdal, "and you cannot possibly succeed."

"Thanks for the tip," Dylan said, "but this is getting us nowhere. What are you doing here?"

"I am visiting on behalf of your friends," Merdal said.

"Right," said Dylan. "How is that exactly?"

"It is simple. Surrender to me or they die."

"Really? They might disagree."

"I have powers you cannot comprehend," Merdal threatened, "and the deeper you go, the more will die."

The thing that scared Dylan was knowing Merdal was completely correct about not comprehending the extent of his powers. He'd been full of surprises, doing things that supposedly couldn't be done, and Dylan had no idea when he was going to be able to pull another one out of the hat. Maybe something like forcing Dylan out of the Stream of Consciousness, which would be catastrophic. All the same, the way to play it was still cool and unimpressed.

Dylan did his best to maintain the slightly arrogant composure.

"Ah, the old reverse guilt trip," he said. "Look. Whoever you kill is on you. Period. People all around me have been dying like crazy, and they're all on you, you ridiculous moron. Do you expect me to believe that if you could have killed any of us, we wouldn't be dead by now? Nice try on the daubitira, by the way. Biological warfare fail."

"You are a worm," said Merdal, "and you will be crushed."

This is exactly where Dylan wanted Merdal for the moment, distracted by irritation. It was time to leave.

"And you are utterly inconsequential," answered Dylan. "Bye."

Dylan instantly moved both himself and his parmalon to just outside the Zafago, which was still landed near the destroyed buildings. The parmalon had clearly never been transported that way before, and got very excited. Dylan reached for him, to calm him down.

"Easy there, boy," said Dylan. "Everything's fine." The parmalon did seem to react to Dylan's voice, and became less agitated. Dylan got up next to him, with a hand on his neck. "Everything's fine," he repeated. The parmalon settled down, and Dylan put the jar of unlo into one of the saddlebags. He looked past the parmalon to the razed buildings, and the thought crossed his mind that Kof wasn't around to return the animal to any more. It was his now.

The hatch on the Zafago was down, and Dylan rushed up the ramp, leading the parmalon. Freddie and Urbor stood at the top, with two other lenthers.

"Let's get out of here," said Dylan. "Merdal's here."

"Where?" said Freddie.

"Back in the green dirt," Dylan replied. "At least that's where I left him."

Urbor confirmed the hatch was secure, then gave the take-off order.

"What's Merdal doing here?" Freddie asked.

"I don't know," said Dylan. "Trying to scare me, I guess."

"Did it work?"

"Little bit."

"Did he touch you or your parmalon?" said Urbor, remembering all too well the last time he picked up Dylan after a visit by Merdal.

"No—well, not that I know of," said Dylan.

"His methods cannot be known," said Urbor. "There is nothing to do but proceed, and deal with whatever comes when we see it."

The two lenther crewmen began to lead the parmalon away.

"Just a sec," said Dylan. He hung his hat back on the saddle horn, then reached in a bag and pulled out the jar.

"Bingo!" he said.

"Amazing!" said Freddie. "You did it!"

"Outstanding," said Urbor. "Truly outstanding. Congratulations, Dylan."

"Thanks," said Dylan.

"What is it?" Urbor continued.

"Duh—it's unlo," said Dylan.

"Clearly. But what is the nature of the substance?" Urbor said with some playful irritation.

"No idea," Dylan lied. "I got with the Barbadan, and he took me to scoop some of this out of a big cauldron."

Freddie looked at Urbor. "Man, is he a bad liar. It's something totally disgusting."

Urbor nodded. "Bat piss."

"Oh, come on," said Dylan. "Bats? I'm so sure." Freddie and Urbor just looked at him. "Oh, whatever, but you won't believe the real story, either."

They left the dock area and strolled down the corridor as Dylan relayed the events on Rondaka. As he told the story, Dylan realized he was especially gratified to have seen and experienced something Urbor and Freddie knew nothing about. For once, Dylan was teaching them something about the universe. It made him feel like a contributor for a change, instead of just a reactor.

They reached the conference room. The Arbar and Studepron were sitting on the table. Dylan took the jar and set it next to them. The three of them were silent as they stood looking at their prizes.

"You guys thinking what I am?" said Dylan.

"And that is?" said Freddie.

"That it's really insane to have these sitting out here instead of in a safe somewhere," Dylan said.

"It is true," said Urbor. "I confess that part of me was in some sort of denial, even with the guardstone pieces right here in front me, that we were actually collecting the genuine elements of a Kan Pri. No one we have ever known has ever known anyone who has seen any of these, and yet here are all three. And yes, I suddenly find it almost disgraceful that we have not secured them better."

"Well, now that all three are here," said Freddie, "we're only an hour away from using them. And *that* is going to be a singular event."

"Speaking of which," said Dylan. "We never talked about the particulars of actually being successful in getting these. We need to find Xarnicus, right? How do we do that?"

"Nobody finds Xarnicus," said Freddie. "We need him to find us."

"OK," said Dylan, "how do we get him to find us?"

"It is time to gather the Panel," said Urbor.

"Yes, it is," agreed Freddie. "Dylan, come with me to the utility ship. We will take that to Yaku. Urbor can use the exposure bubble."

"What's Yaku?" asked Dylan. So much for teaching Urbor and Freddie about the universe. He was back in eternal question mode.

"Yaku is a temple where the Panel of Xarnicus gathers," said Urbor. "It has been so for billions of years. It is hidden beneath the waters of Carf-Tulali, a world that is ninety percent oceans. It is there that Xarnicus will find us."

"Well, then, let's do it," said Dylan. "Think I'll grab a couple things first. Urbor, you got a bag around here?"

Urbor went to a drawer beneath the bar and produced a drawstring bag eighteen inches long, made of animal hide.

"Ah, perfect," said Dylan. He put the Arbar, Studepron, and unlo inside, along with the Holitaph, which had also been on the table.

"Let's not misplace that, shall we?" said Freddie.

Dylan and Freddie went down to the dock rooms and launched the utility ship, and Freddie immediately transported them through the Stream of Consciousness to Carf-Tulali, hovering a few thousand miles above the deep blue surface.

"There," said Freddie, "we're in a stable orbit. Ready?"

This time, they both flopped to the floor from having been seated in the utility ship. Dylan might have been embarrassed, except that Urbor was the only one there, having already used the Stream from the exposure bubble on the side of the Zafago.

Maybe it was Urbor's use of the word "temple;" maybe it was Dylan's own preconception of a place where the Panel of Xarnicus would gather. Whatever had formed his expectations for Yaku, it did not match them.

Not that it was a bad thing—Dylan's vision of the place was like a palace court, with high ceilings, ornate pillars, and maybe a huge marble table with high-back chairs all around. In reality it was more like a hunting lodge made of natural cut stone blocks, complete with an angled roof with exposed beams, an open area in the middle, and conversational seating around small tables. It was actually kind of homey, a pleasant surprise from the ceremonial surroundings Dylan had in his mind.

Dylan and Freddie got to their feet. Freddie and Urbor stood next to each other and said a few odd words together. Within a few seconds, other beings began popping into the room. It was an eclectic collection of creatures. Skin, fur, scales, feathers; red, yellow, brown, green; short, tall, thin, round; arms, legs, wings, horns. Soon there were twelve in the room, including Dylan, but then it stopped.

Dylan leaned over to Freddie. "I thought you said there were always twenty in the Panel of Xarnicus," he said.

"I also said they cannot all appear in your spatial dimensions," said Freddie.

"Right, right," said Dylan.

There was a buzz building, but Urbor raised his hand and it stopped.

"My dear and honored friends," Urbor announced. "I give you Dylan Bruce."

There was an immediate uproar of applause, and shouts of "Well done!" and "Hear, hear!" and "Burba kikik!"

Dylan was overwhelmed.

This was not at all what he was expecting, and it hit him at a deep emotional level, soaking in everything he had been through and realizing that the Panel members were doing so as well, from Dylan's consciousness through the Stream.

This was the Panel of Xarnicus. These were the guardians of the ways of the Ancient Guard. Some of these beings were probably tens or hundreds of millions of years old. And they were applauding him. *They* were applauding *him*. He was too stunned to speak.

"All right, all right," said Freddie. "You'll give him a big head.    Never mind that he's been in the Stream of Consciousness for less than a week, and now has assembled not only the Holitaph, but all three mystical elements of a Kan Pri, probably for the first time in the memory of anyone but the Ancient Guard themselves." The room erupted with more applause and cheers.

Just as it began to subside, it turned to gasps as Merdal appeared in the middle of the room. He began to laugh.

"Oh, don't stop on my account," Merdal said. "That's right. Some of you have already noticed you cannot leave. I have perfected perhaps my greatest sorcery. And the simplest. I have surrounded this place with a field that suppresses the Stream of Consciousness. Everyone is trapped here, except me, of course." He pointed a tentacle at Dylan. "And you. How convenient that it was so easy to allow your bonding with the Holitaph to set the stage for this fitting climax."

With his other two tentacles, he held up a red box the size of a basketball. "This is a bomb. Simple and effective. It will detonate in fifty seconds.    Dylan, surrender to me this moment and I will defuse it. Defy me, and most of the Panel of Xarnicus will no longer exist."

Dylan did not hesitate for even a moment.

"I defy you," said Dylan. "And I challenge you. Meet me in the green dirt of Rondaka. You know the place."

He disappeared.

Dylan was among the dark green rocks where he had last met his foe. Instantly, Merdal appeared ten feet in front of him.

"Odd, I call this surrender," Merdal said as he wrapped a tentacle around Dylan's ankle.

Dylan moved himself fifty feet away. Merdal appeared again before him.

"You have no time to play such games," said Merdal, reaching again for Dylan.

Again Dylan moved; again Merdal followed.

"I will—"

Dylan's timing was perfect. This time, when he moved, he also moved a large number of the Rondakan rocks into a wide ring fifteen feet over his head, with Dylan standing below the center opening. The rocks immediately fell all around him, and Merdal had much too little time to react before he was crushed.

Dylan saw a tentacle between the rocks, shriveling and dissolving into nothing, as he had remembered seeing Thergon perish in the parking lot at work.

He had six seconds.

He appeared at Yaku, grabbed the bomb, moved it into deep space, and returned to Yaku, with two seconds to spare.

The room again erupted into applause and cheers. Dylan was rightly congratulated on his focused resourcefulness, and the Panel members each extended their personal thanks for saving their lives. Some celebrated right away by transporting out and back into the room, to prove for themselves that the field suppressing the Stream had died with Merdal.

For his part, Dylan could scarcely believe he had actually done it. He was amazed at himself and his frame of mind, so open and sharp in these past days. Although in his own head he was chalking it up to the influence of the Holitaph, it still felt invigorating and satisfying to behave that way.

Dylan was feeling like a contributor again, and could really scarcely believe he was hob-knobbing with these beings. They spoke to him without airs, in relaxed conversation as friends, asking Dylan what the green dirt of Rondaka was like, and the Barbadan, and the creature who peed in the sand. It would be impossible to assemble a room full of people who had done more or known more about the universe than this crowd, yet not one of them had been where Dylan had.

It was a remarkable feeling.

Freddie was getting his own recognition from the group, too, and that made Dylan happy. Freddie had been assigned by the Panel to keep Dylan safe, so Dylan's success was Freddie's, too, which he readily shared with Urbor. Urbor, for his own part, had saved Dylan's life at least twice, and the Zafago and its crew were a critical part of their success.

"All right," shouted Urbor, "it is time. Dylan, would you do the honors, please."

Dylan was happy to, but wasn't entirely sure what Urbor meant by that. "And that would be?"

"It is time to make our presence known to Xarnicus," Urbor said. "When the Studepron is placed in the Arbar, and the Arbar filled with unlo, Xarnicus will visit to complete the ritual."

"Ah," said Dylan. He pulled a small table out toward the open space a little, and placed his drawstring bag on top of it. He reached in and removed the Arbar. The room became abuzz with subdued chatter. Most in the room had never seen guardstone before, and none had seen the Arbar in person. The excitement was like a group of kids watching the newest toy go on display.

Dylan reached into the bag and pulled out the Studepron. More ooh's and ah's. Dylan was smiling so hard he was about to give himself a cramp.

He reached in and removed the jar of unlo, to scattered applause and general enthusiasm.

Finally, he reached in one more time and held up the Holitaph. Emotions ran high, but the noise in the room died down. It was as if this moment in which these four items were together struck everyone at once again, and they were simply in awe. They were overwhelmed to realize not only that these legendary items they had been told about by the Ancient Guard for, in some cases, millions of years, actually existed, but that they were all in the same place at the same time.

Dylan wasn't sure exactly how this should go, but he had an idea. He knew well they had all heard and read and passed stories about these things, and here they were. Dylan had seen enough to know that mystical rituals sometimes destroyed the artifacts used to bring them about, and it would be a serious shame if any of these things were gone before anyone really saw or touched them.

He backed away from the table a couple steps.

"Before we use these," Dylan announced, "you guys should take a second and admire them. The guardstone is really incredible stuff. There's time to appreciate them before the ritual."

The group was surprised and extremely grateful as they crowded around the table, passing the items between them. They looked, smelled, and caressed with a combination of excitement and reverence, like schoolboys trading baseball cards that were all hall-of-famers.

This went on with energy for a couple of minutes, then, seemingly all at once, they acted like it was suddenly foolish to be fawning over these things, and they gently put them down and moved back a bit.

Dylan was ready to proceed, and feeling privileged but uncertain as to just how this should go. He looked at Freddie. "Is there some special way to do this?"

"Nope," said Freddie. "The items have their characteristics, and they'll take care of it."

"All righty, then," said Dylan. He picked up the Studepron and laid it gently into the Arbar. Guardstone being what it was, there was no cause to be gentle, other than the overall ritualistic feel of it. He picked up the jar of unlo, screwed open the top, and shook the wet sand out into the Arbar. Just because he felt like it, he took the Studepron and wiggled it a little, so the unlo was distributed all around it.

Everyone instinctively took a step back from the table and held their breath.

# CHAPTER 20

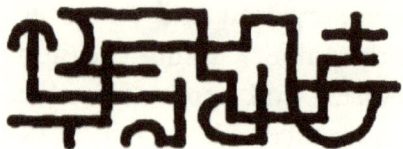

Within the surprisingly comfortable underwater confines of the hunting lodge that had served since time immemorial as the temple of the Panel of Xarnicus, what happened next was a feeling unlike anything Dylan had experienced before.

The Arbar began to glow, but not with just light. It glowed with a sort of warm energy Dylan could feel in the Stream of Consciousness, and he knew this was what Xarnicus would feel and follow.

A few seconds later, a being appeared next to the table and directly in front of Dylan, about three feet away and facing him. It was fairly large, about the size of a pony, with the appearance of a lizard. It looked much like a wingless dragon.

It was Xarnicus.

Xarnicus did not wait for any reaction to his appearance. "Greetings to you all," he said. "None of you have seen or met me, yet for untold generations, you have stood ready to protect that which I and my brethren have represented since the early days of the universe. For that I thank you more deeply than my life could express. We are forever honored."

The moment was beyond description, and the reaction was spontaneous. The Panel broke into applause. Not the cheery, congratulatory applause. This was applause from respect, admiration, and brotherhood.

It even sounded different. They were applauding not only Xarnicus himself, but his presence. They were applauding themselves.

They applauded the moment, the circumstance, the memory of all past members of the Panel of Xarnicus.

It was emotionally overwhelming.

Almost as striking as the applause itself was the feeling that there was nothing to say as it dissipated. No one in that room could have dreamed of this day, and now that it was here, it felt as if it was already fully experienced. There was nothing to add.

After a silent minute that felt intensely reverent and in no way awkward, Xarnicus spoke.

"Now, with deep regret, I must ask you all to leave me with Dylan. The transfer of the Holitaph is for him alone. Thank you again, my magnificent friends and brothers."

Without a word, the room emptied.

Xarnicus looked at Dylan. "You, my friend, have shown me valor and honor and sacrifice, to go with courage, cunning, and resourcefulness. Freddie told you the Holitaph was providing you with clarity and focus. While true, the Holitaph cannot create those properties or instill anything you do not already possess. It can only magnify and enhance what exists in you. All you have found the personal strength to accomplish has been through your own resolve, your own focus, your own character, amplified through the enhancement. In many ways, you were your own Holitaph."

"May I speak?" said Dylan.

"Of course," said Xarnicus. "I am old. I'm not God."

"This experience is beyond the unbelievable. No imagination could create what I've seen in these recent days. "

Dylan looked Xarnicus squarely in the eye.

"Thank you, said Dylan. "There's no point in saying it any differently than that. Thank you for being who and what you are, so that the friends I've made had occasion to share their time with me."

"You are most welcome, Dylan Bruce," Xarnicus said. "And for being a most worthy friend to them, you shall be rewarded. Now, we have business."

"Yes," said Dylan.

"Hold the Holitaph," said Xarnicus. Dylan took a step to the table and picked it up. "In the presence of the mystical artifacts, the Arbar and Studepron, adorned with unlo, we are prepared to perform the Kan Pri."

"What do I do?" said Dylan.

"I will speak the words of the Kan Pri," said Xarnicus, "then you will know what to do."

"Very well," Dylan said.

Xarnicus closed his eyes. "Purva tempada krovanik."

Dylan was intrigued that these words were not English, realizing that they had some mystical properties that defied translation through the Stream. Oddly, it wasn't until this moment that he also realized that had been true of the "burba kikik" phrase all along.

On hearing these new words, Dylan felt a warm rush through his body as Xarnicus opened his eyes again and raised one of his front feet, with the palm up. Dylan placed the Holitaph there, and held it there so they were both touching it.

"Burba kikik," Dylan said. His hand burned just a little as he lifted it away.

"It is now my turn to thank you, Dylan," said Xarnicus. "All shall be as it was, and all shall be remembered."

◄ ■ ►

Dylan was walking away from his car in the middle of the parking lot at work. Quite startled, he stopped and quickly looked all around, then up at the autumn morning sky. No police tape. No pile of dirt. No destroyed office building.

Also no Xarnicus, and no Holitaph.

No Freddie, no Urbor, no Zafago.

Dylan ran out to the curb and looked down the street. All normal. The collapsed warehouse two blocks down was there, standing. No lightning ball burn marks in the grass. It was looking like time had reverted back to the beginning. But he remembered everything.

*Can Xarnicus really do that?* "*All shall be as it was, and all shall be remembered.*" *He turned back time, but left my memories of the entire thing. Wow!*

The last time around, Thergon had already come out of the ground and given him the Holitaph by now.

No Thergon. No Holitaph.

*What does that mean? That the Holitaph wasn't stolen in this new timeline?*

He walked across the parking lot toward his office, thinking about all the things that could be different now. There could be any number of reasons Thergon wasn't there. He wasn't dying, and transported himself to the right destination. Or he died sooner, and couldn't bond the Holitaph with anyone. He was wondering and worrying and driving himself crazy, all before he even got to the building doors.

Dylan opened the doors and went inside. Everything still looked normal. He made his way through the maze of cubicles. When he got near his, he saw his colleague, Matt Claremore, in the cubicle next to his.

"Brian stopped by for you," said Matt.

Dylan was slightly tentative, going through this as if he expected Merdal to come crashing through the roof. "OK," he said.

"Ready for the review?" Matt said.

"Review?"

"The design review with Chancellor Engineering today?"

said Matt.

*Oh, right, that's what was happening while I was sitting in Freddie's underwater dome.*

"Um, yeah," said Dylan. "Close as we ever get, I s'pose."

"Right," said Matt with a chuckle.

Dylan took off his hat and coat and hung them on his cubicle wall hook. He sat at his desk and hit the button to boot up his computer. This was just surreal. And the weirdest part was that not long ago, this was more normal than even your average normal. Now it was this reality that was surreal.

He went to the kitchenette nearby and got a cup of coffee.

*Well, it's not Andalatarian millis, but I do like coffee.*

A couple other people ambled by, trading greetings. All normal.

He got back to his desk; his computer was still booting. The security software they put on the company machines now practically crippled them. He picked up a file from a stack to his left. Notes from a failure investigation on a deficient component placement process.

*This is what I used to do? Yeah, I guess it was.*

His computer was ready. The first thing he opened up was always his email. It initialized, and the new emails popped onto the list on his screen. The one it defaulted to began with "Hello, Bruce." He hated that, but it happened all the time. With two first names, his showed up on everyone's computer as "Bruce, Dylan," and it was shameful how many people couldn't bother to switch them around.

He decided not to read that one.

*Screw 'em if they can't get my name right.*

He scrolled down a few, and a curious one caught his eye. The subject field read, "Tuesday on the Zafago." He clicked it immediately. It read:

> Dylan,
> Welcome to the Stream! Curious thing—there's never been a former Holitaph owner before. Not a

live one, anyway. Looks like you get to keep your exclusive membership in the five-dimensioned club. What do you think of this fabulous new timeline? In this one, Merdal is still stuck in the fourteenth dimension, and the Holitaph is still safely with Xarnicus. Cool, huh? No quest out here now, so don't quit your day job. See you soon!

Freddie

Dylan was so distracted by the new environment, he just assumed the Holitaph was gone and he wasn't in the Stream, so he hadn't even considered trying to use it. In a split second, he felt it. He moved his coffee cup into his hand, then back to the desk.

*This is unbelievable! I'm not the only one who remembers it all—we all do, and I'm still in the Stream of Consciousness. Xarnicus is amazing!*

A completely new frame of mind quickly swept over him. He read the email again, to take in everything Freddie was saying. It answered some questions, to be sure, but it also sent a message. Freddie was telling Dylan not to go overboard running around the universe instead of earning a living. He did still have a life to support.

Dylan understood that, but all the same, this transformed everything about his attitude.

As Xarnicus had said, in his focus and his mental capabilities, he was his own Holitaph.

Just by having done what he'd done, being connected in that way, he knew no design review was going to be mundane ever again. There were no other humans in the Stream of Consciousness, but that was OK. There was plenty of fun to be had without abandoning everything he knew of life.

The universe would still be there.

# CHAPTER 21

D ylan was relaxing in a lawn chair. He reached to his side with a pair of tongs and lifted an exquisitely charred hot dog off his portable grill. He nestled it in a bun and dribbled some ketchup over it. The roar of the waterfall was the perfect backdrop as Dylan took a juicy bite and looked out from his vantage point on the mountainside just outside the mouth of his favorite cave, on Verwen.

"So, this is a hot dog," said Faldra, lounging in a chaise next to Dylan. She held up the specimen he'd prepared for her and looked it over for a moment, then took a generous bite of her own and chewed a few times. "Mm. This is fabulous!"

Dylan gazed over the gnarled trees and soothing river valley, and the deep red mountain range to his left. "Yes, it certainly is."

◁ ■ ▷

www.ingramcontent.com/pod-product-compliance
Lightning Source LLC
Chambersburg PA
CBHW032005240626
47153CB00003B/1126